Todd Sherman's

OBSCURDITIES

OTHER WORKS BY TODD SHERMAN

Pitching Ice Cubes at the Sun: a Book of the Dead

Opals for Libras

Kong Hong

Paralytic States

Fluid Babies

Rise, Osiris!

Phlogistics of a Simple Man

TODD SHERMAN'S

Obscurdities

Book Art & Design: Melissa Hindle-Sherman

ISBN: 1533527636
ISBN-13: 978-1533527639

To Gareth Liddiard and The Drones.
Your music makes me want to be a better writer.

Contents Absurd

Not While We're Mortals

What would you do to attain immortality?

Five figures in robes around a large dining room table had long ago asked this question of themselves. And one more, too, for whom the five were waiting in fidgets and flutters. Each cowled face regarded the other — sought out the tiny fires in eyes kindled by this singular passion. To live forever. At whatever cost. And then maybe? To rule.

As Eshmun, Melqart, Asherah, Anat and Qetesh. And Hadad to come. Old gods' mantels wrapping the bones of a newer century. In a black circle with a fireplace stoked into blazing majesty. Mystery. Smoke up the flue with the secrets to the rites to the dark pageant that would ensure eternal survival. Of the fittest. The most fecund. The farthest reaches of this watery planet would weep at the feet of these grand new deities speckled in ancient dust. And from downturned frowns those godheads would blot out the searing eye of the sun and bring crushing sandals upon those puny, milk-fed, mortal heads.

"Where is Hadad?" said Asherah.

"I got a message," said Eshmun. "A temporary delay. He should be here any minute."

"Has he forgotten how important this day is?" said Qetesh.

"Stay your tongue!" said Eshmun.

And now five would-be gods shuffled their feet. Thick hoods hid red faces. Melqart fiddled with a curved blade on the table.

"Molekh?" Anat pointed at a bowl.

"It's the traditional spelling," Melqart said.

"Moloch is the traditional spelling," Anat said. "M-O-L-O-C-H."

"What's it matter?" Eshmun said. "The intent's the thing."

"Then how about I call you Assman?" She thumbed to Melqart, still messing with the knife. "And him Milk Fart?"

Eshmun threw back his hood. His shorn hair had a long piece of blue lint in it. His evil eye failed to do anything about this. But then, he was unaware of its presence. Else he would have surely burnt it into oblivion.

"A bowl is a bowl," said Asherah. "I mean, we're content with burning dolls in effigy."

"Oh God, no," said Qetesh. "It took weeks to get that burnt plastic smell out from last time."

"I brought a straw one," Melqart said, looking at the floor. "Just in case."

"Straw or plastic, what's it matter?" And now Anat's hood back, too, revealing flowing ebon waves. "If Moloch is spelled Molekh. How do we know we won't summon some obscure demon who'll just run around with his little red peter shooting semen all over the place?"

"Jesus," said Asherah. But she wouldn't reveal her face. "A bit extreme, isn't it, Anat?"

Anat whipped on her. "Shut your virgin hole."

"Virgin?" said Asherah.

"Virgin?" said Melqart, looking up briefly.

"Don't derail the proceedings," said Eshmun. "This is so you, so totally true to form. Every damn time, Anat."

"Go fuck a steak knife," she said.

And more shuffling since the other three—Asherah, Melqart, Qetesh—knew that Eshmun's red-stained brow was only one insult away from blowing this cramped little room to kingdom-never-come. So now Qetesh pushed back fabric from a buzz cut. Like Eshmun's except without the lint. And she had lashes nearly thick and long enough to bat away that blue string from over that yet-reddened visage.

"Should we just start without Hadad?" she said.

Qetesh looked to Asherah who looked to Eshmun who looked to Anat who looked to Melqart who looked to the floor as if a face with eyes and breath of a dragon resided somewhere below.

"Take off your goddamned hood, Malcolm," Anat said to Melqart.

"Anat!" said Qetesh.

And Asherah silently brushed back her own. Twining crimson snakes. Flames to frame wintry perfection. Fire and ice and wringing her flushed hands.

"No human names," Eshmun said. "You know the law."

"Shove a carrot up your tight ass, Edmund," she said.

"Oh, you'd like that, wouldn't you?" Eshmun said.

"I can change the spelling to MOLOCH," Melqart said.

"Shut up," Eshmun and Anat said at the same time.

Qetesh walked to Eshmun, braving his burning stare, and picked the lint out of his hair with thin fingers. She went to Melqart and unfolded his cowl. Their eyes met and he nodded. She patted his thick brown curls and returned to her place in the circle. She turned to Anat.

"Happy now?" she said.

Anat looked at the ceiling and shrugged.

"Let me stoke the fire," Asherah said.

"The fire's fine," said Eshmun.

And so they all stayed put. Melqart almost reached up to fondle the hilt of the knife again. But he didn't. Eshmun was still red as blood from a fresh kill. Anat's eyes still beheld the wonders hovering somewhere beyond the white spackled vault. Asherah licked her fat lips while Qetesh whisked out those scouring lashes. And

Molekh on the bowl would forever be Molekh. An eternity wouldn't erase that hand-painted stain.

The sound of a door opening and the flames from the fireplace flicked out toward those in the room. The sound of the door closing. And heavy tread. The last robed member to appear. Cowled and carrying a wicker basket. He set it gently on the table and gazed around the room. All eyes on the tall dark form outside the circle.

"I've arrived," he said.

"No shit," said Anat.

Eshmun held out his hand. "At last brother."

They shook.

"Hadad," Qetesh said. "You've kept us."

"I'm deeply sorry," he said, hand to chest and slightly bowing.

"I brought the bowl this time," Melqart said.

Hadad squinted at it. "It's spelled wrong."

Melqart's face dropped.

"No matter," Hadad said. "It's the thought that counts."

"It's not a fucking Christmas gift," Anat said.

And Hadad laughed. He patted the bowed handle of the basket on the table.

"But I have brought a gift," he said.

Eshmun leant in and peered, but the contents were concealed beneath purple felt.

"The fire's going out," Hadad said, pointing.

Asherah ran to the hearth, grabbed the poker, and stabbed at the orange heart until it flared its anger in a glowing tongue.

"What have you brought?" said Qetesh.

Hadad waved her to him. "See for yourself."

She stepped forward, blinked at Hadad, hesitated.

Hadad laughed again and tossed back his hood. "So long as everyone else is doing it." And he ran his palm over Qetesh's shorn scalp. A perfectly even dome. "What a lovely bowl your skull would make, dear Qetesh."

"Well," said Anat, "if you're finished fingering the sweet young thing."

She strode up to the basket and whipped off the blanket, for blanket it was. It's called a blanket when it's covering a baby. For that's exactly what was in that wide wicker bottom. A sleeping baby with its pudgy arms out to the sides.

"What the hell?" Anat said.

"Shhh," Hadad said. "It's sleeping."

"I can see it's fucking sleeping," Anat said. "But why is it sleeping in here?" Her arms out. "In this room. In this house."

"Wait," Asherah said.

Asherah dropped the poker. Eshmun dropped his jaw. Hadad dropped his hand. And Melqart couldn't drop his head any more than it already was.

"Why do you have a baby?" Qetesh said.

"Couldn't find a babysitter," Hadad said.

Asherah stormed forward. Now wishing she still held that poker.

"No, no, no," she said. "You can't. We can't. I won't."

"Won't what?" Qetesh said.

"Hadad . . ." Eshmun said.

"Holy fuck, Harry," Anat said.

"What?"

Eshmun swallowed hard. "She's been using our real names. Just generally being a pain in the—"

"Forget that," Asherah said. "Edmund." Hard glaring. And she pointed round the room. "Malcolm," at Melqart. "Katrina," at Qetesh. "Emma," at Anat. "Harry," at Hadad. And balling up her fists. "Harry, what have you done?"

"Well, Abigail, since the spell's been broken," Hadad said. "We're going to kill this baby."

"Like hell you are."

Asherah pounded back to retrieve the poker.

Hadad cleared his throat.

"For hell we are," he said. "All of us. Not just me." His head swung to everyone. "We're all in this together."

"I didn't sign on for this," Eshmun said.

"Pussy," Anat said.

Asherah came back like lightning. And like lightning, too, her eyes. Cracked bolts blistering the very air. She swung the poker at Hadad and he sidestepped.

"Whoa, Asherah," Hadad said. "There's a baby here."

"Would offering a baby to Molekh bring us eternity?" Melqart said from the corner.

Asherah flared at him and swung the poker again and this time it landed.

"Not if you don't spell Moloch right," Anat said.

Asherah spun. "You think this is funny?"

Anat smiled and crossed her arms. "Actually . . ."

"Ladies, ladies," Hadad said. "This is not the way to comport yourself before a sacrifice to Moloch or Molekh or however everyone decides we want to spell it." He patted the wicker handle again and put a finger to his lips. "And if we wake this little lamb we're going to have a whole lot of fuss for nothing."

"Fuss?" Asherah said.

"Jesus, Asherah," Qetesh said. "Stop being so melodramatic."

"Are you telling me you approve of this?" Asherah said. "That you could take that baby's life to extend your own?"

"Well," Qetesh said. "The fake ones aren't doing us any good. And that reek after." She wrinkled her nose.

"And how do you think burning baby's going to smell?" Asherah said.

"Pretty tasty, I should think," said Anat.

Asherah threw the rod at Anat and she caught it. Actually caught it. Maybe the effigies had given some measure of power after all. And the greater strength a real

16

live human could accord brought Anat's pink tongue out flicking on those blood-plumped lips.

"Look, I understand," Hadad said. "I don't really want to kill the little bugger. But," and he twisted his own lips, "if it makes me a god, I'm all for sacrificing a whole truckload of babies."

"I think there's a joke in that," Anat said.

Eshmun coughed. "I'm with Asherah on this."

"Pussy."

"Yeah, yeah, you said that."

"Not enough, apparently."

"Enough for me."

"The only thing that's enough for you is that carrot," Anat said. "Remember?"

And Eshmun shut up. Hadad cleared his throat. As preface to a speech, maybe. But that pontification was cut short.

"I'm in," said Melqart.

"What?"

Asherah goggled. For the second time, most likely, wishing she had that poker.

"Yeah," Qetesh said. "If it's got to be done, it's got to be done." She wrinkled her nose again. "I just don't want to be the one to do it."

"You're a pussy, too," said Anat.

"Damn straight," Qetesh said. "Vagina all the way."

"I knew it."

"You're not using a carrot on me."

"Once you go anal," Anat said, "you never go back."

"You disgust me."

"So then," Hadad said. "That's four for and two against. We've got to come to some consensus on this."

Eshmun shook his head. "There's no way I can do this. I'd rather be dead."

Hadad put his hand to Eshmun's shoulder. "Come

17

on now, man. This is what we've been working toward all these years. Enough of the empty rituals and silent responses. Enough of the games and pretense. Let's do this thing for real. Let's do this right. No more pussyfooting around. No more straw men. No more Cabbage Patch Kids. Enough infantile balking. This time we make it count." He waited for Eshmun to meet his gaze, hand still to shoulder. "Let's kill this baby." He rubbed the tensed muscle. "Come on, friend. It's for all of us. Don't be selfish."

Eshmun dropped the gaze and cleared his throat again. Asherah went straight to him. Threw off Hadad's hand. Stood square at Eshmun and tried to find the defiance between those cracking eyes. Cracking because tears were forming. Tears forming and ready to slip like his resolve.

"We can't do this," Asherah said, digging into the pupils.

Eshmun tried to speak. Opened and closed his mouth several times.

"Stop bullying him," Anat said.

"Eshmun," Asherah said, not turning around. "We can't kill a baby. We can't."

"I know," he said.

"See." Asherah smiled.

"But we must."

"We mustn't."

"I don't want to die."

"Neither does that baby." And she pointed back to the basket, gaze unwavering.

"It's still sleeping." A tear fell from Eshmun's cheek. "It'll never know."

Hadad stepped forward. Tried to put himself between Asherah and Eshmun. But Asherah pushed as mightily as her small frame would allow, crimson snakes out biting, and Hadad fell back a couple paces. He put out his hands. But she was back at Eshmun.

18

"Look at me," she said. "Look at me, Eshmun."

And he looked.

"This baby could grow up to be one of us," she said. "He could one day be a god."

Seeing but not seeing.

"Let's grab some snot-nosed brat from the mall," she said. "But not this innocent baby."

"That's just it," Eshmun said, spilling rivers down those blotched cheeks. "The innocence."

"So you agree with me?"

"That's why we have to do it."

Asherah's eyes reflected the ragged claws from the fireplace—the swinging carmine curls at her temples. She grabbed the knife from the table and Eshmun just blubbered.

"What a baby," Anat said.

"Asherah," said Hadad.

But Asherah had taken the knife, holding it out crosswise—hilt in one hand, curved tip flat in the other—and presented it to Eshmun. But he didn't move. So she pressed against his chest with a bow.

"Take it," she said.

Eshmun swung those watering pools among the other members, but any answers there died out on blood-gorged lips, flailed away by lashes, choked by the wrinkles of brows, lost in the shadows under eyes that flickered from the hearth's searing heart.

"You want it so bad," she said. "You do it."

"I'm not sure I can," he said.

"Pussy," one last time from Anat.

The orbs of Eshmun instantly hardened. The black stones beneath the seas rose from those depths. Onyx monoliths. Subsiding waters. And runic messages etched somewhere along the shiny surfaces to kill! kill! kill! So Eshmun raised his hands to accept the blade.

"You're leaving me alone on this?" Asherah said.

Eshmun didn't even nod.

"I'm ready," he said. "Give me the blade."

And Asherah flipped that knife with her wrist and sunk it to the widest arc of the blade into Eshmun's heart. The crinkles around his eyes tightened and collapsed. He spit up blood. He fell to his knees, then to the floorboards on his side, hilt sticking out and flouncing with each of his kicks. Asherah backed away from the spreading scarlet pool.

"What have you done?" Hadad said.

And Melqart started screaming. The baby, awakened, bawled it's eyes out. Outscreamed Melqart. A baby can do that when it isn't stabbed and thrown into fire.

"Great," Anat said. "Now what do we do?"

Hadad stepped forward. "You really set us back, Asherah."

"What can I say?" she said. "He was weak."

Hadad turned to Melqart. "Will you stop your caterwauling and be a man." He waved at the table. "Get the bowl and fill it with Eshmun's blood."

"What?" Anat said.

Hadad shrugged. "We can't let it go to waste. Moloch is waiting."

"But he's not an innocent," Anat said. "The things I've done to that man with a carrot."

"I've got a hacksaw in the basement," Qetesh said, and ran out the room.

Hadad bent to Eshmun's twitchless body and extracted the knife. He wiped the edge on his robe and stood up. He handed it hilt first to Asherah.

"Well, my dear," he said. "Get to work."

Melqart had flipped the body over and was squeegeeing blood from the floor with his hand into the bowl. Anat stepped to Asherah, looked at her and smiled.

"That was pretty ballsy of you," she said. "Stupid but ballsy. Especially for a virgin."

"God," Asherah said. "Will you give it a rest? I've

fucked everyone here but you."

Anat's eyes popped. "Well."

Hadad stabbed at the air with his finger. "Grab a leg each, ladies."

Qetesh rushed back into the room with the hacksaw in hand. She paused at the sight of Asherah's red hair dangling and Anat's ebon locks, inches from the thick puddle, robes smeared at the knees, spreading apart Eshmun's legs like a wishbone.

"I can't do this part," Qetesh said. "Blood makes me woozy."

Hadad grabbed the basket with the baby and thrust it into her arms. "Then shut this thing up."

"What do I do with it?"

"I don't know," Hadad said. "Take it upstairs and rock it to sleep or something."

Qetesh nodding. "I can do that, I can do that."

Hadad had taken the saw. Qetesh whisked again from the room, cradling the basket to her chest, the backs of her pixie ears stinging red. Footsteps clomping up a stairwell as Hadad handed the saw to Anat.

"So," Anat said.

Looking into Asherah's face of concentration. Sawteeth ready to bite above a naked ankle. Anat tucked a black tress behind an ear.

"How you feel about carrots?" she said.

And we'll leave that question for Asherah to finish.

For there was a question put to you, the reader, at the beginning of the story. About the lengths one would go to gain immortality. And the answer? It doesn't matter, since we're all going to fucking die anyway.

But the baby upstairs? At least its unstabbed heart will beat on a little longer.

Play With Your Ass

Balaam makes for Moab. God is pissed. Sends an angel.

Really? That's how you're going to start this?

So Balthazar stops reading before he's barely begun. Head up and probing empty space above the kitchen table. And why the kitchen table? Why not on the couch or in a cradling chair or at least at his computer desk propped at a forty-five degree angle? And why not just write 45°?

Thought the angel was supposed to come at the end of the narrative, he says. Not at the very beginning.

And there's a blinding light like a cosmic ray burning through the blinds. Yes, from his kitchen window. And, yes, he's now looking, squinting actually, out that window. What a cliché. As if the angel were about to appear. So back to the paper on the cracked oak table.

The donkey sees the angel with sword and turns off into a field.

Seems a bit abrupt, Balthazar says, for the angel to show up with the sword first thing.

Kind of ruins the climax, says a voice.

Balthazar starts back, eyes goggling at luminescence in humanlike skin hovering at the back wall. He swallows human spit and blinks human lids, Balthazar does, as if it will make the apparition more palpable; coughs a human cough and clears a human throat, Balthazar does, as if those hackneyed devices would dispel that floating being, or at the very least bring naked feet to naked floor; opens a human mouth and scratches the furthest arc of his human head, Balthazar does, to rub the otherworldly impression into his very human brain and so mix with the reality of the most banal of kitchens. To temporize infinity. Or some such shit. But it didn't help that the cosmic glare through the window washed the being in an ocean outside of time. Outside of earth. And yet here it was. And here it spoke.

Do not go any further.

But I'm sitting down, Balthazar says.

Do not turn another page.

I've only read two lines.

Do not go to Moab.

Moab? Balthazar says. Is that the new bar downtown?

No, don't read until that section of the play, it says. It only gets worse.

I don't know. Balthazar raised his hands toward the being. I mean, you're here now, and that was a bit unexpected.

But that isn't. The being pointed to the manuscript on the table. You get to Moab and Balaam goes back and forth between Balak and three mountaintops only to say the same thing. And it's so close to the original source that, not only is it just as dull, but it's flat-out plagiarism.

Balthazar took a sip of his water on the table just beyond the much-maligned papers. He set the glass back down. Shuffled the pages. Ahem hemmed. Cocked his head. Basically, any kind of usual beat that separates dialogue.

Are you an angel? he says.

Yes, the angel says.

And are you going to kill me?

The angel look confused for a moment, a human-spanned moment, but then regained his supernatural composure and held aloft his prodigious sword. And, of course, it glinted from the sun. Through the window, always through the window, because where else can light come from inside a room without a skylight?

You mean this? the angel says. Sorry about that. And he laid it crosswise on the table opposite from the water, the manuscript and the blinking human. I just have nowhere to put this thing. Really gets in the way.

Why are you here? Balthazar says.

Why are you reading that abysmal play?

Because a friend gave it to me to proofread.

Some friend.

Well, I said I would.

And I said you should stop.

Balthazar let his eyes roll around the room. He wanted to get up and check the other rooms but he didn't much relish getting slit like a hog on a hook. So more water went down his throat, the same throat that he just couldn't seem to clear, the very same fragile pipe that had once let vibrate the promise, weeks ago, to a friend that it would be a pleasure to give Balaam's Error the once over.

What are you looking for? the angel says.

The ass, Balthazar says. I'd imagine it will show up, too, if you're here.

Really? The angel crossed his mighty arms. You make this too easy.

Well, it stands to reason that if I'm "Balaam" in this scenario, and you've already made a dramatic entry, then the belated donkey of fable should be loping around any minute now.

You're the ass, you ninny.

I'm the ass?

The angel pointed a cold blue finger. And that's Balaam. That unreadable dreck under your chin.

And so, uncomprehending, Balthazar lowered his gaze to that unfortunately placed play of plays and read the first line that came to him.

Goes to remote height. God gives him a word.

Yeah, it's pretty awful, Balthazar says. It's like it's cobbled together from notes.

It's lies, the angel says.

Well, I don't know about that.

It never went down like that.

Wait, you're saying this actually happened?

I'm saying it never happened.

What never happened?

The story.

In the play?

In real life, the angel says. In the past.

Balthazar put his arms out.

Well, of course it didn't happen, he says. It's in the Bible. Just like Noah didn't build an ark and Jonah didn't swallow a whale.

You mean the whale swallowed Jonah.

Did that really happen?

No, the angel says. I mean that Jonah couldn't swallow a whale.

Oh sure, Balthazar says. That's more preposterous.

I think we're getting off track here.

You're the one who told me not to go to Moab—not to read on. He shrugged a human shrug that even an angel could understand. So now what?

I just want the record straight, the angel says. God actually loved Balak. Thought he was the tits.

The tits? Do angels talk like that?

This one does.

Tits and ass, Balthazar says. Good Lord.

Don't curse.

Balthazar hit the glass of water again. About one third full. Or 1/3 rather. Have to keep track of that so that Balthazar isn't pulling swigs of oxygen later in the story. And Balthazar really just wanted to close those blinds because the light off the angel was hurting his eyes.

Who the heck is Balak?

You can say hell, the angel says.

Who the hell is Balak?

Have you even read the story?

Of course not, Balthazar says. You won't leave me the fuck alone.

Let's not get carried away with the expletives.

Balthazar rolled his eyes. He pushed the papers forward with his fingers.

You want to proofread this thing? he says.

Hell, no.

So Balthazar went back to the humpbacked words on the disfigured pages lying on a table scratched from the implements of previous owners. He scanned the lines. Flipped the pages. Tried to find anything to do with Balak. The angel was all: What did I tell you? Do not go on! I'm warning you. All the time that beast of a sword lying untouched on the table.

Build me seven altars here, ready seven bulls and seven rams.

And so Balthazar read those words aloud.

Well, yeah, admittedly, the angel says. That's not so bad a line.

And when silence was the only thing to hover outside of the streaming light between Balthazar and the hovering angel, that very inhuman being had to release a very human sigh.

But it doesn't lead to anything, the angel says. He just keeps cursing the Moabites and other Canaanite tribes and blesses the Israelites instead.

Isn't it a Hebrew story?

Well, yeah, but so is Jonah swallowing the whale, the angel says.

You mean the whale swallowing Jonah.

Right, right.

So then, what's the big deal?

As the Germans say: Vas deferens?

What?

Vas?

Balthazar shook his head. Drained the last third (1/3) of the glass so he wouldn't have to keep track of it anymore. He cleared his throat one last time. Literally, one last time, I swear.

I am really confused by the point of all this, Balthazar says.

You mind if I stand? the angel says. My aura is killing me.

By all means.

And the angel did just that. And his ankles cracked as he closed his eyes and breathed out deeply. Then he opened his eyes and spoke. But just because he was on his feet, dirtying those heavenly digits and soles on Balthazar's unswept floor, didn't mean that he'd lost the seraphic timbre to his voice.

To just tell the same old story, the same old lie, he says, is more repugnant to me than revisionist history. At least new lies keep you interested.

OK.

I mean, Balaam gets killed at the end by Moses, anyway, when living among the Midianites. So he's not a good guy.

Whoa! Spoiler alert, man.

Oh, yeah. The angel looked down. Sorry.

Man, that's not cool. Balthazar almost reached for that empty glass of water. Now how am I supposed to give this thing an objective read?

It's crap, anyway, man. Like I said.

You know what?

And the sun had gone down enough to stop streaming through the blinds. Or had hit a cloud. Or hitched a ride on a passenger jet since that was more interesting than hanging around an angel standing in a human's kitchen. In any case, the angel was no longer bedazzled. And Balthazar was no longer amused. He pointed out the doorway.

It's time for you to go, he says.

But—

No, no. It's too late for that.

The angel raised his eyes but Balthazar was shaking his head. Still pointing. And not clearing his throat because he'd used up his final one. So the angel slumped, turned and dragged his feet away.

Wait! Balthazar says. Take that goddamn thing with you. He waved at the sword.

You shouldn't take the Lord's name in vain.

Go fuck a donkey, Balthazar says. If you've got the genitalia for it.

The angel didn't look up. Just pulled that weighty weapon off the table and hobbled out the room. The light beamed back through the blinds. Balthazar buried his nose back into the play.

Where was I?

The angel stands in a narrow place. Donkey can't turn. Lays down.

So Balthazar broke a rule and cleared his throat.

Jesus, this thing is shit.

Full Bodies Wine
By Same Name

You didn't know what you were setting into motion.

And it's understandable since anything so preposterously horrific occurring from so small an error, no matter how purposeful, could never have been predicted. Certainly not from someone with such a lack of imagination as you. For someone with a subversive passive aggression deeper than any possible fanciful flight in dream. Because you sleep like the dreamless. And dream like a pebble before the incoming and outgoing tides. And the tidal pull of the everyday dictates all endeavors — whether small or slightly larger than small. But you're still pretty pathetic.

I know this because I've seen you. And watched you sleep. Fidgetless, placid and oh so mindlessly dull.

For years working in the brick building sectioned into flimsy cubes, the noise of the place buzzing like the six sides of a harshly lit honeycomb. And your minor contribution to that restless cacophony. Scribbling and typing and flipping pages. Reference materials and referenced sites and referential turnings of a phrase. The idioms, in and out like the waves; the morphemes like the stones; the calques like eroded bits of foreign glass; the syntax intact along the horizon where semantics flounce like kites against the puffs in the deep blue sky. But somehow all inside that buzz buzz buzz of the brick building as soundboard.

I know this because I've stood in the very heart of this place. Somewhere close to where the queen rolls in her royal jelly.

And now extra hours in this manmade hive. Partly due to cutbacks. Partly due to an increased portfolio. So why no rehires or new hires or maybe being more selective of clientele? You asked this. I heard you. Everyone heard you. But its meaning was lost in the stridulation. The rock crying out as the wave crashed and engulfed it. So you toiled on with more and more banal entries that needed translated. To have attained the fluency of four languages only to render a French business card into English. And no end to the string of the most pedestrian of things flayed out like fish on that beach and deciphered by ancient augurs in stiff white shirts: labels, packages, brochures, catalogues, manuals, hardware, software, help files, user guides, websites, flyers, newsletters, corporate letters, logos, go go going on on on. Buzz buzz buzz.

You knew it wasn't the Rosetta Stone. Not the Coffin Texts from the Middle Kingdom. But surely you weren't prepared for such numbing necessity. You should have been. Or at least slipped into it naturally, being one clipped segment of that flatlined buzz.

If you say et cetera enough, maybe you'll achieve some trance-like state on some far-flung planet with a family of moons that race so quickly on their orbits that they achieve also their own trance-like state. And the next and the next and the next. Triple droned and triple stoned on the pebbled stretch before the receding tide.

And so now you've got your chance at revenge. Rebellion. Revolution. In the form of a brand new customer with very old-timey labels on bottles of garnatxa from Spain. But of course the country is redundant with that spelling, right? Oh linguists and their little games. No wonder no one laughs at your jokes. But soon they'll be laughing—they'll all be laughing. Except for the ones upon whom the trick had been played. The owners of the bottles. Of the wine in the bottles. The producers. And the agency that owned the big brick building:

Babel Ling Brooks Translation

How to interpret the description of a full-bodied wine that goes by the very same name in that very same description? By the letter or in the spirit? Or not at all. Tortured into nothingese. Nonsensical palaver on a tea-stained label for a posh purveyor of affordable Spanish reds. Well, Catalan, technically. But who's going to finish that revolution? Certainly no one before the labels are glued to glass and stuffed in boxes and shipped around the world to puzzle those brave or bored or pedantic enough to read the back of the bottle.

Full bodies wine by same name.

Oh glorious mistranslation! Oh misbegotten bastard! Oh miscarriage of interpretive justice!

You stifled a laugh with the fingers that had penned that abortion. Your shoulders hunched and your chair rolled back from the desk. But those miniature screams against the establishment were subsumed in the hive's resounding, rebuzzing echo. No one knew. And no one would know until it was too late. If it got past the printers. But they only check the settings. They're experts of their own insect kingdom. Don't even understand the chatter of bees, honeyed or otherwise. Because they're ants. And ants only know work work work. Which translates to buzz buzz buzz, oddly enough. Oh you and your little, pathetic, squeaking jokes.

So days had gone by with no effect. Like you hadn't deliberately mistranslated text at all. Like you'd done nothing at all. Maybe going unnoticed if you'd only written a string of Xs and Os kissing and hugging their way to the bottom edge of the label. And you kept going back into that throbbing hive, of course, because you've got bills to pay, and walked down the halls into the inner sanctum, of course, because you had a duty to perform, and you sat in that flat-cushioned chair, of course, because you were only a drone after all, and you put your head in your hands because you'd never been a dreamer.

Was that Supertramp playing in the background? you wonder. But the true wonder is how you can just shrug it off, hum along to the buzz that flutters in decibels just a shade higher than the collective hive heartbeat. You shrug it off and so add that scraping sound of wings to the white noise of the everyday. Today, tomorrow, until the colony dies off and a new queen marks a new kingdom to rule. Supersedure. But would anyone ever hear it? you wonder. No wonder since you'd not be in the ball stinging the queen—not be part of the insurrection. Your head would be in your hands in the chair in the room in the building bricked up from the untranslated.

But you did assassinate a phrase. You did take a Brutus stab at usurpation. And then with blood on the blade you set your butt back in that chair. How can you stand it? Or sit it, rather.

Quite simply, you can't. Yet you must. And so at lunchtime you obey the muted klaxon like the rest of the honeyed mass and head back down the hall, down the stairs out the door, blinking into the wash of light glinting from the panes of all the serried towers ranged round. The home buzz a memory in the head. The foraging bees set adrift on the world's wind. Pollen seekers who must return to the hive with baskets full of bee glue. Bellies full of food.

But beaches have no flowers. So why are you scouting the rocky wastelands?

Maybe because there's the pull of something. Ocean sucking back in on itself. The core of the earth as a giant magnet. The loose bits above slowly sliding toward the center. All navigation in a frenzy. Flight disrupted and grounded and crashing into each other. Crashing. CRASH!

The sound of collapsing metal. Collapsing glass. Collapsing air between crashing objects. Colony collapse disorder. To see the cee cee dee in resulting mangled objects. Crushed cars. But no bodies. Where have they gone? you wonder. And wonder, too, at all the red liquid staining tarmac and dented metal flanks and muzzles of beasts stuck grotesquely together.

Then another explosion of glass. And another. Another!

You turn your head and see a body before slipping into CCD. One body, wingless human, hovering over concrete, reflecting in mirrors of the towers splashed with ChromaFlair paint. UV glowing, a buzzing, growing an aura before a hiss then gigantic pop! Exploding in a spray of blood and glass. Humanoid shards raining from the skies. As other bodies lift off sidewalks in mock rapture and levitate with goggling eyes and glowing skin before the pop! Cars careen into cars as hail hits their growling faces and flanks. Roaring beasts and pop! pop! popping beings. Crimson explosions in the air, kissed by the sun's keen cutting rays, blessed in a fan of red wine, bathing pavement and people yet unlifted in purpled sacrilege. In pinot noir. No! Garnacha. Garnatxa with an X.

Full bodies wine by same name!

And you'd started this, you realized. And the realization sets your feet arunning. Through bloody cataracts and buckshot. Past cars in idle, in smashed union, parked at unpaid meters. Through the throng of uplifted faces, too lately ducking as another pop! sends human debris out in waves. And now screaming themselves as they feel their feet grate and slip into the air. Pop!

And you screaming, too. Racing through that crowd of the gratefully grounded. Sidestepping the dangling legs of the unfortunately elevated. Hands over head to defend against shrapnel. Hands on head, hands on head, oh dreamless dreamer. But at least you're not in the chair.

Pop! Pop! Pop!

Full bodies wine by same name!

But no one heeds you. No one can guess that it

had been you who had unleashed this absurd doom. You and your misstep in the hive of the translators causing the world of humans to raise up and blow into starbursts of bloody red wine. Red, red wine.

Cue the song, you fool. To the soundtrack of this disaster.

And your disaster as you feel your feet get light. Filled with helium, maybe. You beat at the air with your arms, useless wings, no stinger to stick into earth and anchor your ill-omened existence. The little that is left of it. Just one bottle of wine. Seven hundred and fifty milliliters. Five and a half quarts of blood. And as you spin in the air from your futile attempts to right yourself, the visage of another being appears, scared poopless, yet popless, and heating up enough to make the teeth glow.

What have I done? you say.

And the man only blinks before popping into nonexistence. Nothingese.

I'm so sorry, you say.

Your streaming tears mean nothing to the woman beside you. In the air, too, and glowing. And your tears have dried up from the heat anyway. As you look out with drying eyes at the human Zeppelins dotting the ruddy vista. Blowing out one by one by one. Like bulbs full of blood. Full-bodied with high acidity. High viscosity, heavy mouthfeel. And you can taste it, can't you? You can taste the terroir in the terror. The year of that terror. The reign of blood. Because you'd been the one who'd affixed that doomed mistranslation on the label. With the year in black type. And just beneath the paper and the glue and the glass — underneath the skin and bone . . .

The bloody massacre after a failed rebellion.

You swing your arms and spin like an astronaut in space. A bee in zero gravity. A heavy soul now but with a lightened body. At least the bottle. Since the wine was mulled and heated to boiling. And it could not be contained anymore. No paper label could ever stop an explosion.

And so now you're wondering what if you hadn't done it. Hadn't made your paltry effort at individuality. What if you'd instead kept your bloodless fingers wrapped around your droning head in that chair in the hive? What if you'd done nothing but simply translated the line:

Full-bodied wine by the same name?
Well, you've not long to consider the question.
As the colony around you goes, so go you.
Pop!

The City and Its Tower

or

What Was Babel

(Two men in a downtown bar in America. The city doesn't matter. The bar does.)

NIMROD: Fancy meeting you here.
ASHUR: What's fancy about it?
NIMROD: No, I mean what are the chances?
ASHUR: Good, I should think.
N: Bon chance?
A: What's luck got to do with it?
N: I think we got off on the wrong foot.
A: Well, thank God we've got two then.
N: What's God got to do with it?
A: Forget I said anything about Him.
N: Can't now, can I, that you've brought him up? It's like a spectre floating above our heads.
A: Like the sword of Damocles.
N: Like the boulder over Tantalus.
A: At least we're not pushing it like Sisyphus.
N: Can we start over?
A: Why not?

(One man exits the bar. The other walks to the far wall. It doesn't matter who reenters. Only that they meet again.)

NIMROD: How's it going?
ASHUR: Well, everything's still running by Newton's laws of motion, if that's what you mean.
NIMROD: That's not what I mean.
ASHUR: Thermodynamics?

N: Who said anything about that?
A: You asked how things were going.
N: I think this is getting out of control.
A: Entropy?
N: Sure.
A: No, Ashur.
N: God, you're a Nimrod.
A: No, you are. And now you've brought up God.
N: Oh, God.
A: See?
N: Try again?
A: The stone ain't going to roll itself.

(The other man departs. The one who hadn't left before. The other one repairs to the back wall. The one who hadn't before. But none of it matters. Except that they come together again.)

NIMROD: It's been a long time, friend.
ASHUR: No it hasn't. It's literally been seconds.
NIMROD: But it feels like forever.
ASHUR: Ahh . . . relativity.
N: So to speak.
A: Then why say it?
N: Why say what?
A: That it's been a long time.
N: Because that's what people do.
A: Which people?
N: You, me, them. Everyone.
A: Oh, right, right. Relativity.
N: So then you say . . . ?
A: Why do I have to say anything? I don't know you.
N: Yes you do. I'm Nimrod.
A: And I'm Ashur.

(They shake.)

46

ASHUR: So now what?

NIMROD: I think it was my turn to speak.

ASHUR: It was?

NIMROD: Sure was, Ashur.

A: Well, I feel like a downright nincompoop, Nimrod. My apologies. I didn't realize we were having a conversation.

N: What do you call what we're doing now?

A: Ahh . . . letting the laws of motion play out?

N: Should we start again?

A: But we've already shaken.

N: So we did.

A: And exchanged names.

N: That too.

A: So we just keep going?

N: Not perpetually.

A: Oh, God no, that would violate Newton's second law.

N: Ashur.

A: Nimrod?

N: You did it again.

A: Oops. God.

N: Another go?

A: I don't want to walk outside again.

N: I don't want to go to the far side of the room again.

A: How about we just turn around?

N: And then face each other again?

A: Exactly.

N: Let's shake on it.

A: Aren't we past all that?

N: Right. On the count of three. One.

A: Two.

N: Three.

(Both men turn around. They face each other again. It

47

doesn't matter which side they're on.)

    ASHUR: I'm supposed to have the last line.
    NIMROD: What?
    ASHUR: You stepped all over it with your "three".
    NIMROD: Sorry.
    A: I should say.
    N: Count to three again in unison?
    A: I think it only fitting. There are three laws of
motion after all.
    N & A: One, two, three.

(One-eighty, one-eighty again. Who went slightly more
than one-eighty degrees isn't the issue. All that matters is
that they are facing each other anew.)

    NIMROD: So how'd you get the name Ashur?
    ASHUR: How'd you get the name Nimrod?
    NIMROD: Fair enough.
    ASHUR: A fair exchange.
    N: I suppose it has something to do with the tower
of Babel.
    A: You mean Baybell.
    N: How did I say it?
    A: Babble.
    N: But that's how it's pronounced.
    A: The Oxford English Dictionary would beg to
differ.
    N: The New Oxford American lists both
pronunciations.
    A: Who the hell uses that as a reference?
    N: Well, we're not in England, after all, Mr. Ashur
Oxford.
    A: It doesn't matter where you stand. Babel is still
pronounced baybell.
    N: Babble.
    A: Babel like table.

N: Babel like you're a babbling idiot.

A: No need to get nasty.

N: Well, you don't have get all hoity-toity.

A: Hoity-toity is a funny word.

N: Hoity-toity is a funny word.

(They shake.)

ASHUR: What happened to my last line?

NIMROD: Sorry. I did it again. Just get worked up when people don't know their history is all.

ASHUR: Excuse me?

NIMROD: "Therefore it was called Babel, because there the LORD confused the language of all the earth." Balal means to confuse in the original Hebrew. It was a pun. At least some scholars think so.

A: That's linguistics, you Ninny, not history.

N: History schmistory.

A: That's racist.

N: I'm Jewish.

A: Your name would suggest otherwise.

N: And Ashur rhymes with "for sure" since you can never admit when you're wrong.

A: Yes I can.

N: Then do it.

A: Admit I'm wrong when I'm not?

N: In Semitic Akkadian it was Bab-il for Gate of God.

A: That's oversimplification.

N: But not inaccurate.

A: Actually, it was more likely Bab-ilani for Gate of the Gods.

N: But no one knows for sure, Ashur.

A: That's true, my Nimrodundant friend.

N: The original word may be lost.

A: Like Sumer.

N: Like summer before fall.

A: Like the fall of the Roman Empire.

N: Isaac Babel.

A: Babel Fish.

N: Babel starring Brad Pitt.

A: Babel the language magazine.

N: Babel and sons.

A: You mean Mumford.

N: Mum's the word.

A: Mummery!

N: You know, the name is somehow a translation of the Sumerian city Ka-dingir-ra.

A: And balal doesn't necessarily mean to confuse in such a way as to bring about chaos. It also means "to mix". A mixing of languages, maybe.

N: Agree to disagree on the whole thing?

A: Never!

N: God, you don't give an inch.

A: You said God!

N: One more time?

A: You think it critical?

N: We need a resolution.

A: Well, than I resolve to end this.

N: Spin?

A: Spin.

(They nod and spin. And spin back. It doesn't matter who was right on the Babel argument. Only that they were talking. And maybe not even that, come to think of it.)

NIMROD: You know, Etemenanki is a funny word.

ASHUR: So is ziggurat.

NIMROD: "Temple of the foundation of heaven and earth." Goodness, me!

ASHUR: What's so good about it?

N: Nothing.

A: Nothing indeed.

N: Pure nonsense.
A: Drivel.
N: Bosh!
A: Balderdash!
N: Inanity!
A: Outrecuidance!
N: Rubbish!
A: Pishposh!

(They stared at each other.)

NIMROD: So then we're done?
ASHUR: We're done.
NIMROD: Good talk.
ASHUR: Best I've had in years.
N: You're exaggerating.
A: I'm lying.
N: You're standing.
A: Touché.
N: Touch.
A: Ouch.

(They nod.)

NIMROD: Good day to you then.
ASHUR: What's good about it?
NIMROD: Newton's first law of motion.

(Nimrod spins on heels and walks out the bar. Which bar it doesn't matter. But Ashur is left standing in that same matterless bar.)

ASHUR: You bastard! You took my line.

Empurpled

The last arc of the sun slips beneath the horizon and a small city is washed in crimson. For a few spare moments, humans amble and gambol and peddle down streets growing ever crepuscular. Cars pass up and down and are gone. A shout from a parent with the storm door propped open, scanning the sidewalks for tardy children, waving them toward the house with frenzy and one last glance at the cloud-curdling sky before the gate to the inner sanctum can be sealed. Streetlights blink on and the tarmac bleeds like crushed red grapes from invisible feet of . . . The Purpling.

There's this neighbor. Across the corner from me. In a house I can only see two sides of. At an intersection of one-ways. Cars can go up and to the left. From my perspective. But from his it would be . . . well, I don't know what his perspective would be. Not even entirely sure the guy is human. Or the pair of them, more properly, since there's a woman, too. Maybe his wife. I don't know how they do things. But in any case, east and north, to be more precise. So the cars can only go in two directions, but the people walking can go whichever way they choose. And sometimes that's down the middle of the street. Especially when passing by my neighbor's house. Give it a wide berth. A healthy distance from that diseased domicile. Bristling with bacteria, I swear. And maybe that's what they are—a confederacy of a billion organisms alien to our world. Alien to our species. Alien, maybe, to our space and time. And so swinging far from that trap set for unwitting, skipping children. At least they think they can fool the children. But they're wrong. Oh so wrong! Since the kids glide right by. Bikes and skateboards jumping the curb and winging into the street. Even cars hug the right white line. Swear someone will sideswipe a parked car one of these days.

So let's call the guy Rayleigh. Don't know his real name. And the wife Violet. The Scatterings. Seems appropriate since they can only be seen at twilight. For real, I mean. Sure they're out in the daytime when the sun's shining white and hot. Moving around just like everyone else, except they're always clad in purple. That's right—purple. He wears these black leggings under jean shorts and immaculately white tennis shoes. One of those Euro cycling caps. You know, the ones with the small brims stuck up. Maybe Belgian or something. In any case, all that weird get up with a purple t-shirt. Purple, that's the key. And Violet, too, has equally strange accoutrement. Cream Capris and one of those white Mexican blouses with the embroidered top and shoulders. She must have a million of them, I'm telling you. And a wide-brimmed gardening hat and throwaway plastic flip-flops. But the sunglasses, the sunglasses, of course, have purple lenses. So bright they beam the air about like restless lasers. And they're always like this. Oh sure, endless variations to their human costumes. But always somewhere that touch of purple. In the glasses, or in the shirt, or else a scarf or pair of kneepads. I know, right? These Scatterings are really strange.

OK, OK, so they're not really the "Scatterings". Not really Rayleigh and Violet. But so what? I'm not going up and asking their names. They just act too damn weird. I mean, take how they water the trees. Sure they shoot at the roots and soak the lawn around pretty good. But they also spray the hell off the side of the house. Just the one side, mind you. And spray water directly through the window screens without even flinching or batting an eye. Not that I'd see her do that since she's always got on those glasses. And the trees, too. Where the hell did they come from? Just popped up one day—freshly turned soil in circles around those skinny trunks. I didn't hear any digging. The flowers, too. Whole beds of them bright and blooming and sticking their purple petals to the passersby like blowguns. Of course they're purple. What else? And if she's watering the bejesus out of the flowers or trees or side of the house, he's right there with her—watching. She'll move down to the next window and pump a few gallons into their nest and he'll sidle right next to her. And so on and so on until they get to the end, because they only do the one side, like I've said. It's just weird, man. But what's even stranger is how he walks away when the task is done. Or anytime he walks, really. He kind of lopes like a gazelle that's been tranked just before it hits dirt. And if he's got on the kneepads, it just makes the movements that much more awkward. Awkward isn't quite the right word. More alien. That's it. Just way out of this world for sure. And she moves about in an equally strange fashion. Just flits like a bee with wings on one side. So she kind of hops and flutters in circles until she gets where she wants to be. And when they're both out "walking", it seems more like some extraterrestrial episode of Nat Geo WILD than anything earthborn.

But it's not just these external oddities of Rayleigh and Violet that keep me on edge. It's some kind of presence almost being shed in heat waves from their house. From within. As if the home were some kind of nucleus of energy not meant to be contained within those thin walls. Maybe that's what all that hosed water is for— to keep the damn place from overheating and going supernova. Take out the whole block, I swear. My house with it. And that pulsing presence almost has a consciousness. Like a great breathing spirit that hangs unseen above that house — above the north side of this city. Above the trees that swing from a wind that I can't feel, even on my porch, and yet those tops are moving as if fleeing vengeful poltergeists. Sometimes it keeps me up at night. I can hear the restless shake of the treetops. Can hear sheet metal buckling from an unseen force. Can hear the beams of my house creaking like I'm on a ship in the North Atlantic. So I go to the window but can't see a thing except the dampened glow of the streetlamps. Or if it's day, I only see ordinary life wending its way about this city, unknowing of the terror bristling from that pale blue house with the purple flowers on the corner.

Yes, I said terror. Sometimes scares the piss straight out of me. There are moments when I think I see the silhouette of Rayleigh or Violet at the window and it just hits me in the guts. I look again but nothing's there. Or else it had left. But it doesn't matter because I'm running for the toilet. Forgive me for being crass, but it's true. I've been losing weight since they moved in a few months ago. Keep pissing and shitting my bulk down the drain. And I'm trying to pack on the calories. Trying to put that weight back on. But it just slips away. Every time I see that fuzzy shadow at the window and then wisp away. Like they know I know who they are. Even though I don't. Not really. But at least suspect that I suspect. And that's enough to scare the shit out of me. Because when I see those dark shapes within the window frame, it's not entirely human. At least it doesn't appear to stand so. Like it's a shadow from being lifted on coil after coil of gargantuan tentacles. Maybe they stretch to the basement. Well, not basement, since we don't have those here. But to the fetid earth below. Where the glowing nuclear heart keeps cephalopod bodies warm far beneath the lawns and sidewalks and streets. And maybe they're not heads and eyes that look back at me from the windows before I can catch them. Just shuffling limbs passing apertures like portholes on a vessel stranded at sea. And those limbs

58

ready to poke into the holes of every home on both streets extending from my intersection. It's no wonder I'm losing weight!

And sleep. Haven't had a decent night of shut-eye since they arrived. For all the howling of the dogs. Nearly every night. I go outside and scan the darkness for what could've disturbed them. The house catty-corner is silent. No cars or pedestrians. Barely any lights in any of the houses. Mostly dead eyes and stilled breaths. And then something will set a dog off barking again. Maybe it's not from something going by. Maybe it's from something coming up. Maybe tentacular limbs have grown thick and long and strong enough to bust through concrete and swipe at canine legs. Squirming like a deck-landed squid and the dog backing away. Not that I'd know. Haven't seen it myself. Just imaging the scenario that could cause such unimaginable panic. It's got to be worse than what I'm even thinking, right? And I can't be the only one who thinks it. I'll have to get people together. Some kind of neighborhood watch thing. Band us all together. Because something's not right with all that howling. Rayleigh and Violet will probably want to join. No way. No way in hell, man. It's all I can do just to keep food down now.

And so now, peering over my shoulder, out through the blinds of my own window in the dining room. It's daytime. No shadows in the windows. No show today in purple accessories and native dances. Walkers skirting the porch. Cars going north and cars going east. No howling nor parents out scouring for truant offspring. Hours, grateful hours, before the sun must set on this city. On this block that's been invaded by the most unfathomable mystery. An unspoken menace. Something to be avoided but not dug into. But I can't take it anymore. Some kind of investigation must be run. There's a haunting like the great sprawled wings of a demon. Some monstrous bat. And not just glowering down upon the house. But on all of our houses. I'm telling you, we've got to do something. I know it. I can feel it like the prickling at the back of the hand before you flip it over to reveal the spider. And they're crawling, I'm telling you, they're crawling inside that quiet house, just twisting away for the chance to pounce. And we're sitting here like so much paralyzed prey. Just pissing and shitting our existences into a void. Day after day. Night after night. And the dogs howls aren't enough. I tell you —

Wait! They're at their door. And looking this way. Shit! I've got to go.

The sun's flaming head is pushed toward the bowels of the earth. Exiled and soon to be forgotten as the final blood rays slip down the sky. People walk dogs in the twilight and those dogs bark at an impending storm. But not a storm of nature. Not rain on the wind with the promise of black-skied shuddering. Something supernatural. Extranatural. Something draped in the unholy cloak of a votary of Satan. And the kiss of massacres puckering the very air. Wet smacks of gory dreams perpetrated under cover of . . . The Purpling.

So I switched from diet soda to regular cola. Can't keep the weight on, like I've said, so I'm consuming as many calories as I can. Just excreting like I caught some tropical bug and my body's failing at dislodging the infestation. You should see my fridge. The thing's packed with Coke and beer and wine. Sweet wine. Sweet heavy stouts. It's rare that I don't have a can or bottle or glass within quick reach. And passing from room to room in a sweaty haze. I turned the air on but it's hardly made a difference. I've got fans in every room going at all times.

But I'm leaving the windows and doors shut, I'll tell you. Can't give them any chance to sniff me out. Probably leaking off me in gallons—the fear. Fear of the unknown. Fear of what I do know. Fear of what I think I know. But I won't be the mouse that scurries in the underbrush just when the hawk's flying overhead. They don't need any help, the Scatterings. I don't even see birds fly over their way. Never seen them perched on the roof or porch. Haven't seen any squirrels or cats, come to think of it, either. Maybe they'd been there in the beginning, soon after they'd moved in, since the presence hadn't yet taken root. No warning. Just slowly disappearing wildlife in a neat little circle around their property. Except for the flowers and trees, of course. I think those things live on blood or something. Maybe they snatch birds from the sky at night when the rest of us are sleeping. Or supposed to be sleeping, rather, since I can't lay down any longer than the time it takes me to soak through my pillow with sweat. I'm scared shitless, I tell you. And wasting away. And barely eating now, because nothing will stay down. While my teeth ache from all the sugar. Gums sensitive and starting to bleed.

So when a knock on my door pulled me from my pacing to the peephole, I was grateful beyond belief to espy a grinning neighbor. I whipped open the door. "Hey, Luther," I said, "I've been meaning to see you." "Man," he said, "you don't look so good." "Quick," I said, "come in." And I grabbed his arm and pulled him inside. Slammed the door with back to it and panting. "Jesus, it's cold in here," he said. "Would you like a drink? Soda, beer, wine. Creamer." "Creamer?" "Yeah, it helps keep on the calories." And he stared at me funny. Like I was in secret concert with the purple-clad neighbors. "Aren't you having problems keeping weight on?" I said. "Why should I be?" I shrugged. "Maybe your metabolism's different," I said. "What, 'cause I'm black?" I shook my head. "What? No, no, just because people are different." And I was sweating.

Literally, a drop fell from an ear. But it wasn't because of the accusation. I just couldn't stop. "Man," he said, "I'm just fucking with you." And he smiled. So I smiled. I think. I hope it looked natural because I sure as shit didn't feel like smiling. "So," he said, "just help myself?" "Sure, sure," I said, following him to the kitchen. "Take whatever you want." "Goddamn, that's a lot of soda and beer." "There's more in the pantry." "What are you, expecting a flood?" He pulled out a can of Coke and cracked it. "And what's with the temperature? How can you sweat in this? I almost want to crawl inside the fridge." "You know," I said, "that's not a half-bad idea." Shaking a finger, too. Like on a set of a sixties Hammer film. Except there was no clear enemy. Or no clear identity as to those enemies since we know damn well where they are, right? "Haven't seen you around in a while," Luther said. And I kept shaking my finger because there wasn't a director to yell Cut! at the end of the scene. To end it before I shook myself into nonexistence. "Have you noticed anything weird happening lately? Like within the last couple of months." He ducked back into the fridge and returned with a fresh can for me, placing it in my hand, the one with the shaking finger. So I stopped and gripped the can like it was a railing on a frigate. And everything did seem to be tossing about on waves, now that I wasn't pacing. I stopped but the world kept going. Motion sickness, but there wasn't anything to puke up, so I downed the soda instead. "Some cats have gone missing," Luther said.

There was a motion so I whipped my head to the window. I could see the house on the corner sitting quiet and unstirred by breezes. And then refocusing to notice a small lizard working its way down a spindly limb brushing against the side of my house. Poor thing probably fled that evil lair across the way. Maybe sensing the creeping roots under the tarmac and soil twisting toward anything with a heartbeat. No matter how feeble and fleeting. It was safe for now. "Cats?" I said. "Yeah,

Mrs. Lowry had two run off and never come back," Luther said. "And other neighbors, too. And the strays that've been lurking about have disappeared, too." "Then it's already starting," I said and choked on cola. "What is?" "Any children missing?" I wiped tears from my eyes and took another swig. "Children?" "Yeah," I said, "they're bigger than cats. They'd provide far more nourishment." "Come again?" "You know what I mean," I said. "Of course they'd have to move on to bigger prey if they wanted to grow big enough to take over the city." Luther shook his head. "Who?" "The Scatterings." And Luther shrugged, so I pointed out the window to the house on the corner. Shaking finger and everything. "Will you put that down?" Luther said, pressing down on my hand. "You're acting like you're in an old horror movie or something." I shook and clapped my hands, dropping my can. But it was empty. Luther let it roll, maybe didn't dare take his eyes off me. "Horror indeed, dear Luther. But this is no movie." "No," Luther said, "it's poorly written melodrama." "Don't you believe it!" I said. "The Scatterings are gathering power." Luther closed his eyes, but only for a second. "They're not the Scatterings," he said, "they're the . . . well, I don't remember, but they're definitely not called the Scatterings." "See, you don't remember their names." And let that finger have free rein once again. "And that means they've already started taking our memories. Of them at least." "That's absurd." "Obscured," I said, still shaking. "Hidden, certainly, but not absurd." "It's fucking retarded is what it is," Luther said. "And goddamn it, stop it." He pushed down my hand again, but I still felt a jiggling through my whole being. Like a great leviathan was chugging through the waters and ready to stove through the hull and take Luther and I screaming in its unfurled tentacles. "Then what's their names?" I said. "Come on then, man, out with it!" Luther's mouth agape. So he shut it and looked at me with a fixed resolution. I could see it in his eyes. Like he'd only just now realized that I was someone who couldn't be reasoned with. Like how you look at crazy people. Me. Me! "OK, then," I said, "when did they move in?" He stammered and looked away. Maybe rolling the days around in his head and finding out that they didn't add up to anything that could be found on a calendar. "I . . ." I crossed my arms and let my legs take the rocking of the world. "Can't remember exactly," he said. "OK, then, ballpark it for me." His eyes hardened and he shot his gaze at me. "This isn't a game, man." "I know it's now a game," I said. "Games are supposed to be fun. And I'm not having any fun." Luther took me in head to toe. "Looks like you're not having any food either." "Well, you know," and I swept sweat from my brow. "Come to think of it," Luther said, with that hardness eroding before the gales of memory. Forgotten memory because he said, "I can't remember the last time I talked to them. And I know that I have." His gaze drifted through me into the wall beyond. Like he'd forgotten I was there. "I remember the man, the husband . . . what was his name?" "Rayleigh," I said and Luther kept looking at nothing in particular. Or maybe at something specific that he'd rather not have seen again. "He said that he was going to come your house and take down your chimes, that they were driving him mad, going off all hours of the night and day. Like discordant piano strings, he said, popping in fire. That's what he said, like in a fire and breaking with pings that set his teeth on edge." Luther's gaze collected itself and hovered between my eyes. "And he was going to take them down and bury them in the ground so you wouldn't find them, he said, and not for just his sake but for his wife." "He puts a foot on my porch," I said, "and I'll break his arm." "What was her name?" And Luther's eyes connected with mine. "Violet," I said. "Yes, maybe," he said, "no, no, that's not right." "Then what?" I said. He shook his head. Almost as much as I'd been shaking my finger, I swear. So who's being melodramatic now? "I can't even remember when I talked to him," he said, "seems like years." "They haven't been here that long," I said. "I guess," he said. "But at least you remember about the cats," I said. "Cats?" "That they've gone missing." "They have?" "Like Mrs. Lowry's, remember?" "Who's Mrs. Lowry?" "The neighbor." "They're the Scatterings, I thought," he said. And so I reopened the fridge and pulled out a beer. The top popped and handed to my friend who looked about to burst into fits.

A sudden movement and glinting light from a storm door. I looked across the street and saw the woman step out of her house. She flittered in circles down the steps. I was pointing again and phlegm sputtered in my throat for lack of speech. The power taken from me like Luther's memory had been of that woman's real name. "Violet," I said. And Luther turned. And now she was in the center of the road. At the heart of the intersection. And cars weren't bothering to go north or east. And she looked up at us with the purple lenses fulminating like electricity in glass jars. And and and. Always and, because something's always happening that will soon be forgotten by Luther and maybe soon by me, too. And and and until nothing wipes the brain in black felt. And as she stood there flaming out her goggles, I could see that little lizard reappear, scurrying up and down the branch, as if to get away from searing heat, laser-focused and penetrating green skin. And now Luther's hand came up with a shaking finger as the lizard dropped like a displaced brick. "I remember, I remember," he said. "What?" I said. "The coils, the coils," he said. "And?" I said. "Oh my God," he said, "oh my fucking God." And I swallowed a thick ball of spit as Violet slowly raised her skinny white arm and held out a finger toward us as straight and searing as those beams from her glasses. It was all I could do to step to the window and pull the blinds. The whole time my tongue stuttering, my feet shuffling as if aboard a warship in retreat.

Better lock your doors and secure the windows. Bring in your loved ones and beloved pets. Stock up on water, canned goods and ammunition. For the red sun will blink one last time and send bruised fury across the sky to lash brittle houses huddled like tinder before the flame. And that angry wind will whip pilot flames into a raging conflagration. Holocaust. Nothing left in the searing wake except carbon and the sooty footprints of demons on unholy parade. Nothing left–the very memory burned from the molecules. Dirty snowflakes blown by haunted breezes. Best to buy a brand new shovel and dig yourself away from the wasting plague. Dig until your nails bleed. Dig as if your life depended on it, for it does. The shifting feet of devils rains down sand. So keep on digging, mole, dig! dig! dig! For the scattered ashes of what had been the town will soon be washed in wave after wave of . . . The Purpling.

There's a scratching outside the house. I peek through the blinds, the peephole, down airvents and cracks in the ceiling. Can almost feel a heat through the floorboards. Like there's a twisting ball of anacondas below. As if anticipating the advent of some fresh hot evil. Set to fits and ready to burst the very wood. To drag flabby prey to the blazing center of it all—the sweltering heart. Except they'd only get skin and bones. Popping eyes and knobby joints. Because there's barely anything left of me. Can't keep on the weight, like I've said. Leaking through these floorboards. Probably sizzling on the restless snake bodies. Steam and more steam. Creating a greenhouse effect. Proper atmosphere for the horror I know is just waiting mere hundreds of feet away at that house on the corner. Every time I look at the house— behold its silent, funereal stare—it's blank-eyed terror—I can hear the scratching again. I know that's where it's coming from. I know! Can feel the itch raking along my jutting bones. Creep at the touch of a ragged nail running the underside of my skin. My teeth chatter and gums bleed. I'm both hot and cold. Freezing fingers, burning toes. I adjust the AC but it doesn't make anything colder. I stick my head in the freezer but I still hear the scratching. Like something's worked its way out my brain and digging at the skull. I glance in the mirror in the dining room and catch a swaying tentacle. Spin and gape at the window, but it's only the twig clawing at the house. Clawing because it knows what happened to the lizard, maybe. Clawing to get away from the twisting snakes, maybe. Clawing at siding to get my attention, maybe, so it will have one last witness before it's consumed in hellfire. But it's only a twig. And I'm barely more than twig myself. And I'm just itching to shut out that god-awful scrape scrape scraping in my skull. Outside the house. Across the street to the house. That damned domicile with its tongue cut out.

Oh my God, Luther had said. But God had nothing to do with it. And I haven't seen Luther since he'd pointed at horror out the window. Ineffable and mute and pointing back. Eyes of purple flames. Soul as black as a tar pit at night. When it snags the lesser beasts and sucks them into painful oblivion. Suck suck suck at the beasts that dare to tread the tarmac. Unknowing and soon to be unknown. Unremembered. Unrecognizable as anything other than the fetid sludge at the swamp's bottom. Where all the dead leaves and beasts and soot and grime collect into a universal black lump. Like the lump in my throat. And now I hear the scratching at the vocal chords. Oh my God! But there's no God, like I've said. Unless God is that twisting shadowed mass below. Malevolent and restless. And I'm stuck in this house, sweating and shitting and flaking away. All the while there's a churning in the guts. And maybe that's God, because it sure hurts like hell. Or else the blood in the teeth, from the gums too soft to even poke with the tongue. Maybe that's God, the blood, because it sure tastes like hell. Or that emaciated face the stares back at me in the mirror—maybe that's God, because he sure looks like hell.

A knocking. A distant knocking, I swear. So I run to the door but there's no one there. And the scratching. And the scraping. And my feet itch by being inches from heat-maddened vipers. I put my palm to the door, but it's cold. Of course it's cold, I've been blasting the AC for hours or days or weeks. Can't remember. Can't remember when I first woke up in a pool of my own sweat. Just remember that they were there one day, the Scatterings, and that they wouldn't stop watching me even when I tried to ignore their existence. But may as well forget the existence of God when I know he's real because I can see the evidence in the knife-edged cheek bones, the blood on the teeth, the asps in the belly. Know God is as real as the fall of lizards from limbs. As real as the silence that circles the trees and flower beds, the very house itself. The absence of life can be felt as a God, of sorts. And that God laughs and laughs with bloody fucking teeth.

The flowers! Oh, the flowers! There are so many now. Exploding all around the front of the house—around the porch. Like kudzu on trees or ivy climbing walls. Choking and bursting with Tyrian blooms. Royal and electric and pulsing with sentient life. I can feel it, I swear. Can hear voices, somehow, over the scratching. Voices from the blooms that shoot like poisoned darts. Poisoned darts for wayward necks. Stray dogs and cats. Ignorant pigeons and robins and mockingbirds. All one grand mock to the one grand God of nothing nothing nothing staring back from the unreflecting windows of the house on the corner. That goddamned infernal hovel of horror unending. Horror upon horror upon horror until the very words lose meaning. Retain only the rhythm. And that rhythm the sound of one great scratching. The God! The God!

"What are you blathering about in there and you're blathering about?" a voice says. Outside the door.

Though I can't see anyone on the porch. Yet I hear a voice just the same. So I say, "That's my teeth chattering from the frightful cold, I swear." And the voice, "Turn up the heat the heat turned up." And I say, "Are you insane?" The voice, "Tear up the floorboards the boards on the floor all torn." And I scream. Yes, scream. Because something brushed the tenderest spots of my soles. And a laugh. Conflated with another laugh. Or just maybe echoing upon itself. Or maybe just seeming so as it bounces from one drum in my head to the other. Chortling echoes off my soul. "Aren't the flowers pretty the prettiest flowers in the world," the voice says. And I say, "The flowers, oh God!" And it says or they, "God, that's funny you should say that God's funny." And I'm shouting now and pounding on the door. But my skinny fists feel like hammers with splintered handles. "This isn't a game," I say, "there's nothing funny about this." And they laugh and say as I run down the hall into the dining room, "Thank you for removing the chimes you chimed and so we answered."

"NO!!!!!"

That spoken line all alone. Because it was the only sound. At least in my mind. And that defiance was everything. And that everything was nothing. And I knew that nothing to be God. With exclamation points. Lots of them. Because nothing says something louder than too much punctuation after capital letters. What am I talking about? Who's talking? What is this all about? I think I say. But then I thought there was only room for NO!!!!! ON!!!!! and on and on. So I run to the kitchen and grab a knife, yes grab a knife, and hoof it down the hall, yes hoof if over those twisting snakes, and bang on the door again with a fist, yes bang even though I think my arm will shiver to bits, and stab at the door, yes actually stab at the door, just to steel myself for combat with disembodied voices and mocking echoes. I swing the door wide and so, too, swing out that blade. But purple to ribbons with eyes clamped tight and face empurpled. Purple like the flowers across the street from me, when I reopen them. My eyes. A sight of the sky slipping in blood and growing darker. Purple wave upon purple wave. Buckled upon itself as if horror just couldn't wait its proper time to rain down hell from the sky. Scratching and rending itself to pieces just to get at flesh and burst that flesh until all the red spills out and stains porches and asphalt and houses and cars. North and east. Lids shut again from all direction. And swinging that chopper and hitting nothing but nothing and more of—

"Open your eyes your eyes are open," they said.

I don't understand, I tried to say but couldn't.

"Look how beautiful the sky looks robed in purple in purple robes and descending the throne in beauty," they said.

I feel stiff, I tried to say. But I had no throat.

"See the place where you lived you lived in a place that you now can see," they said.

My home is on the wrong side of the street, I tried to say. And felt a scratching. And realized that it was the crawling feet of a bee on my face. And then something shot out and that bee exploded in a purple puff.

"You have shining purpose and that purpose shines on the face of the sun," they said.

You, I tried to say. A loping and a fluttering. Four feet before me. Kneepads and purple thongs. Violet burning lenses look down at me. And I scream scream scream my little petalled head off. That is, if I'd had a voice to scream.

In the space between day's death and night's reincarnation, there is a rush of royal color. Kings and tyrants and emperors. Invasions, torture devices and dungeons. Mantles on shoulders walking through different rooms — those meant for glory as well as for horror. And yet that shade pervades. Blood spilled in the sky or on altars, it's all the same. It deepens and thickens and coats all the living with its taint. Sticks like meat in teeth. Wild spraying fury. And kisses of bloodlust expire before the coming night. So pull close your own mantle about the shoulders. Pull tight and keep wide-eyed for devils howling in the wind. And thank the stars when they finally dot the ebon curtain of night, for you've made it one more day. You've escaped the tightening coils of . . . The Purpling.

Spanking Trade

Listless Larry Lanegan sits in his den of porn, leaning over a laptop with the news blaring and the flies buzzing. Packs of condoms and cock rings and nipple clamps in dismally-lit counter displays. No customers. The only voices from the flat screen across the room whipping unseen paramours into a frenzy. And the voices from the laptop, too, of course. Except more shrill—fewer echoes, fewer appeals to be hit and hit again since those on the broadcast had been pummeled enough by bombing. Or so the reporting went.

But not in The Spanking Trade. Not in this lair of lecherous pursuits promised to be played out once leaving this darkened chamber for another. Dark pursuits. Ass-pounding endeavors. Stretched and prodded and swinging like sides of beef. Larry hardly thought there was enough lube in the place. If he'd given any of it a thought, since he was glued to the LCD, only bothering to glance away when one of those innumerable flies landed on unspanked flesh and irritated him to leather-bedecked reality. And so he grabbed a paddle. But not just any paddle. This was The Spanking Trade after all, and so the object deserves a special sentence:

Paddle Daddy's Unbreakable Spanking Paddle.

And for anyone curious enough to peruse the product details, they'd learn that it was fashioned from clear industrial grade polycarbonate plastic with holes along the body to allow a faster swing and better contact with a vinyl grip to prevent slippage. To prevent slippage. Because everyone knows how embarrassing it is to have a paddle sail across the room mid-spank. You lose face. And worse, all faith from that accusatory face bending its head back toward you. No matter how camel-whipped crimson that ass is. So a vinyl grip glued to shatterproof plastic. To stop the bullets of doubt before they could even be loaded into the chamber. An implement close enough and worthy enough to swat flies. Though Larry knew the Paddle Daddy Pocket Size Leather Spanking Paddle would've been better. They were on reorder. So the flies would have to take the full fury of the Big Bertha of paddles.

The voices on the faraway flat screen spouted approval. Yes, hit 'em, yes, hit 'em good. Again! Again! Hit that bad little bitch again. But Larry had failed to land a single blow. Only succeeding in roiling the air in currents that may have damn near created the perfect atmosphere for cumulus clouds. Such a dank dungeon Larry sat in. And the waves nowhere to go. Buffeting the little buzzers in eddies like Cessnas caught in a twister.

Breaking news on the red banner at the bottom of the laptop's monitor. A tropical storm forming in the Indian Ocean and threatening to go sideways to God knows where. Some master being looming in the sky with a giant human-thwacking paddle. They'd keep him informed, the reporters told Larry. Or all the Larrys of the world stuck in dead-end shifts in brutal trades on stools duct-taped over pleather.

So Larry considered the voices across the room. Only for a moment. Just to corroborate the news from halfway across the world. But, of course, it had all been pre-recorded—all played out in a pageant everyone knew the end to: someone was going to beat someone else's ass. Just that simple. And far too simple for Larry the Listless to pay any more attention to than a fly on the East Coast would give a dark funnel forming in the heart of Texas. And something dire was forming, to be sure. But in this room it was all the same—always the same. Bend over, panties to ankles, skirt flipped up and hand ready to strike the thunderclap of Zeus into blue-veined flesh. Always, always, always the same old objects in the same tired rows on the same static hooks dotting nearly every flat surface in this same humid, choking room: ball gags, bondage cuffs, corsets, spreader bars, strap-ons, dildos, floggers, whips, canes, swings, racks, rope, hoods, clamps, rings, smother boxes and spanking horses. OK, only one smother box and one spanking horse. That kind of equipment was expensive. And they were hard to move. Maybe the owners shouldn't have sprung for the fancier models. Who cares what kind of wood they are? Larry had asked them. Especially when nose is buried in butthole. And they answered that they had a discriminating clientele. Larry had shrugged and they ended on an agreement for a commission on every smother box sold. And Larry had sold exactly none. He did come close once on a spanking horse, but now there's a fly on Larry's eyelashes.

Swat! Swat! Swat!

Got it, the little bastard. Not on his face, of course, or else he'd have been unnecessarily concussed. And then all the flies would really storm his prostrate body. He'd swung the paddle and the black buzzer sputtered to the counter where its tiny body was soon obliterated in a stain by the gods who'd crafted the unbreakable Paddle Daddy.

More news breaking as waves pounded the buildings lining a beach in Sumatra. Footage shot by hovering helicopter. People running through streets and along rooftops. The surge of water rolling like an unforgiving master lashing its servant. Except they weren't in a dungeon. Not strapped to some bondage bed in a private room of a private room. They were in the great wide world getting subsumed by Nature's raging fury. Flattened like bugs on asphalt and disappearing under foam.

Help! Help! Help!

There's no help for you, said a voice on the faraway screen and Larry shook his head. Of course there is, he said, because he knew the scene would end before moving on to another pantomimed season in hell. The only help you'll get is the backside of my hand, they said. And Larry hated it. Right down to the sweating soles of his feet. And you better believe it was sweltering in this dungeon. Somehow it made all the garish gear that much more believable—that much more at home. Where else would an acrylic ball crusher with adjustable screws not seem funny? Well, to Larry, the idea of a ball crusher was always funny. When someone bought one. Yes, those did move. But then again, Larry had never had his own set of tender grapes popped into one of those bad boys. Shudder.

And another fly gets crushed to pulp. He flicked off the mess like a wiper would on a windshield and scanned for more targets. Buzzing about like they owned the place. As if there wasn't a bored employee freshly prodded into action by their prickly climbing feet. The plastic hammer of the gods again and again to the porn shop's counter. A regular carnage. God damn, Larry said, this thing is unbreakable. And whack! whack! again. Good thing about the vinyl grip, because this weapon was getting covered in gore.

A swirling eye now, and a blinding white eyewall with rain bands shimmering unseen by those being destroyed on the surface. Crashing far beyond coasts into the hearts of cities and villages and communes unprepared for such rending violence. Those in cars or boats or bikes alike all caught in the destructive stew, sent to run the speeding currents into other displaced objects until everything smashed into the cast iron side and rang out the doom in waves. The sky torn in squalls and endless howling. From the winds. From the waters. From the people caught in the swell. And that great unblinking eye staring down as if dead and uncaring. Like some monstrous being born of the gods that went blind from all the horror it had perpetrated on those below for aeon after aeon.

I'll tell you when you've had enough, they said faraway, and it was hard for Larry to pull away from the disaster before him. A man in a white shirt rolled up his sleeves and cracked a belt across his palm. Zooming into his face, resting on the eyes, blue flaring irises like circular skies on planets with rotten cores. And of course the bent-over victim hadn't had enough. Not really. All part of the shallow screenplay probably written in another dungeon just as dark as the one in which the man with the belt was standing. Just as dark as the one Larry sat in. Dark and smeared with blood like the paddle. And Larry's balls ached like they'd been in that plastic crusher. Ached to get off that stool and get out that room and never come back.

Thwack! Thwack! Thwack! and now Japan on the laptop suffered — the North Pacific coast. Wham! Wham! Wham! There goes northern Chile. Boom! Boom! Boom! Mindanao, Philippines. Whack! Whack! Whack! Papua New Guinea. Smack! Smack! Smack! Myanmar. Bam! Bam! Bam! India on several fronts. And now Japan again. And again and again. They don't call it the Ring of Fire for nothing.

The amount of dead flies sickened Larry to his tossing stomach. Like when you accidentally walk into a fly strip. He'd never guessed there were so many. So much destruction. Like the field of massive splinters on the laptop. And the people crawling like wingless flies through the wreckage. Downed power lines and upended trucks. Caved-in houses and uprooted trees. Bodies lying bodies crying bodies trying to make sense of all the bodies. And nobody in the room with Larry except the voices and evidence of the massacre he'd wrought.

What have I done? he said.

And from the kindling a great body pulses. It shakes itself to the sea. It rises from the waters and throws off droplets the size of cities. A thundering roar erupts in a human chest. Spitting dragon heads sway from the neck. It rises on coil after coil and those tentacles extend past the very height of the hissing dragons. Fire and fury and smoking in a body of feathers. Shaking the earth to the mantle. Shuddering crust and blasting a host of tsunamis again. Never ending. All consuming. And gigantic enough to reach out, maybe, and palm the searing sun. To blot out all light from the humans. To feel that burn after a leather belt bounces off a plump naked ass. And the welts soon to form will be the only lasting evidence of any destruction. Because our world was shaped by typhoons. The calamitous forces necessary to bring about the next evolution. Just as typhoons are necessary to a slave on the extender. To the fly flattened on transparent plastic. Like listless Larry numb to all the pounding around him. In rocking wave after wave. Nearly lulling him to sleep on that taped-up third-rate stool.

But then a ring of the bell plucks him from the maelstrom. He is set on dry ground to watch the waters recede. In the blazing sun of the light bulb overhead he can witness the white welts like raised beds in a garden. Life again. Life anew.

And a couple walked to the center of the room and turned to Larry. With hand slapping cherry wood and in a strong clear voice the woman said, How much for the smotherbox? So Larry Lanegan hid the grimy paddle under the counter and got off the stool to pound that sale home.

Dick Upstanding

Klaxon Corp. called Richard shortly after his shower. Well, not the corporation exactly, but a representative of the company. And not just any old flunky, but Anassas, queen of the colony, the one with the green eyes who could instill green envy into the most petrified of hearts. But then not a queen really — nor any kind of leader. Except to Richard. She was the be-all and end-all to his code breaking existence for the secret to unlocking her honey dripping heart was the only code he had failed to crack. And now this, too, attendant with the call, an appeal for decoding in a message that had stumped everyone else. Or so she said. And to call direct on the emergency line, and not have sent some fusty troglodyte, meant that whoever in Klaxon had sent her knew that it was only within her power to quicken a slow man to immediate action. She did have that sting, Richard knew, to spur bulls into rampages in fields or kill rats in their nests before the pestilence could spread. She was an upstanding soul and brooked no tolerance for slack-jawed inefficiency. And it was all Richard could do to stop from staring.

"So what makes this time any different?" he said. "You couldn't have gotten one of the others? My shift hasn't started."

Even dripping wet and bereft of coffee he knew what he'd asked was preposterous. Of course. She'd called on the emergency line, after all. Her makeup was applied. Her hair in golden waves spilling beyond the edge of the screen. Her green eyes freshly polished emeralds. And those gems looked sharp enough to slice through any horsehided breastplate a barbarian may wear. Richard wanted to reach through the screen and touch those eyes even though he knew they'd cut him to the bone. Nerves stinging in the air and he just a grateful fool to have had the chance to touch a goddess. Or a queen. Some latter-day Boudica ready to lance any man brazen enough to drag soiled feet through her kingdom. Even if it was only Klaxon Corp.

"One of the NOVAs has been stolen," Anassas said, "and the man with the kill code has disappeared."

"It's useless without the launch codes," he said.

And regretted it. Of course she wouldn't have deigned contact him if there weren't more to the story. More to the story. Ha! He couldn't take his eyes off her long enough to even care. Let them have the NOVA. The only part of the story Richard cared about was how it led to him being graced with the project to brush those waving honeyed locks. Brush and brush and brush and close his eyes to imbibe the ethereal scent. The wind stolen from Parnassus as Anassas had been stolen from the angels. Angels.

"Open your eyes," she said. "Do you think this is a joke?"

"Of course it's not a joke, you wouldn't call me if it were a joke."

Her eyes didn't blink. And Richard was conscious of wetness at the top of his shirt.

"It's not a joke, is it?" And regretted that, too. But he barreled ahead. "Because I don't see what this has got to do with me."

"The launch codes were stolen," she said.

"I assumed as much."

"Which means that the NOVA could be set off and we'd be unable to disarm it."

"I gathered that as well."

He just kept talking so that she had to keep talking

84

because he loved so much how her lips moved. Pink ribbons in which he ached to be tied, choking every inch of his flesh.

"Half of the United States could be wiped out," Anassas said. "You don't care?"

"Depends on which half it is."

"Excuse me?"

"Ever and always," he said.

And now really, really, really regretted even having a tongue to fob off such palaver on someone far too exalted to bend an ear to rat squeak. Because he sure as hell felt fully rat now. Crawling with lice and clicking his incisors. Boring into that soft fleshy part at the base of the neck. What was that called again? Come on Richard, think! think! think! Superb notch that it was, he wanted to bury his nose in it and drink deeply like a landed fish tossed from the boat back into water. Sniff her all the way down to the sternum.

"Are you even awake?" she said.

"I haven't had my coffee."

"Well, then the world will truly come to an end."

"Not as long as you're here."

"I may not be for long." Green stones hardened. "And you may not be either."

"Really?"

"Really."

"But what can I do?" he said. "I'm just a code breaker."

"You have the kill code."

He almost said What? Instead he bit his tongue. Literally. Blood welling and eyes watering. So he didn't have to regret saying something foolish before the queen. But now he regretted not saying something. Anything. Because for her to think he had the code was utter foolishness indeed. And to think that Anassas had said it. Because he didn't have a kill code. Never had a kill code. Never had been deemed important enough to be trusted with one. And he thought he'd never live to see the day when Anassas, the queen, the emerald-eyed beauty squeezed from some golden-halled heaven, would let foolish speech sully those tender lips. Like a stinger in a jar of honey. Oh . . . he shook with the prospect of her jar of honey. He'd sting her, all right. He'd sting her so hard she'd forget ever uttering such inanity to a mere drone.

"So where is it?" she said.

"Where's what?"

"The kill code."

"I don't know," he said. "You said it was stolen."

"And now you have it."

"I really don't know what to say."

And she coughed. A tiny aristocratic cough before leaning in. Jewels out-bedazzling LCD.

"Say that you'll hand it over."

"How can I give you what I don't have?"

"You're wasting time."

"I swear to God I don't know what you're talking about."

"Well, soon enough you can tell him yourself," she said. "Because we're running out of time." She pointed at him. "You're running out of time."

Richard squeezed the back of his head and water came out. Not out of his head, of course, but from his hair. Maybe he was hoping to squeeze out some memory of having been given the kill code. Maybe he'd been drugged. He was pretty groggy. Or else hoped to squeeze out the code itself. Whatever it would take to make him hero for the day. Get in her good graces. Dub him number one fuck drone of the hive with stinger upstanding. And that jolted something.

"Have we ever had sex?" he said.

"Sex? Really? Now? That's what you're thinking of?"

"Well, it's just that," he said, "I almost remembered something. Maybe."

"We've definitely never had sex."

"Member . . . wait a minute."

"We don't have a minute," she said. "And if you don't cough up that kill code, you're about to be stormed by some no-shit, no-joke agents. They'll rip it out of you if they have to."

"Rip it out of me . . ."

"So stop screwing around and give me what I want."

"Out of me . . ."

Anassas put a hand to her ear and looked down. Like she was staring straight at Richard's crotch. And he felt a stirring there he instantly regretted because he knew there was nothing he could do about it. He couldn't thrust himself through the screen. And how embarrassing would it be if the agents kicked in the door and he with a hard-on ready to burst the zipper on his jeans? Oh Lord, he had to adjust himself in the chair.

"They're outside your place now," she said.

"But how do you know I have it?"

"We have a reliable source."

"Who?"

"The agent with the kill code left a recorded message before he disappeared."

"OK."

"They're on your floor," she said. "Give it up. Don't be a dick."

"Oh, come on, now."

"Come on yourself." Her voice acquired the hardness of her eyes. "Come on and give it to me, Dick, before they rip it from your skin."

"Jesus!"

A pounding at the door. A shouted order. The jingling of metal and swish of fabric.

"Look at me, Dick," Anassas said. "Look into my eyes and tell me what I want to hear. I'm the only one here." She flicked the top button to her blouse and Richard saw that milky white divot at her neck redden with desire. "Tell me how bad it hurts and how you need to get it out of you. Tell me, Dick." Leaning in closer. Breaths making her skin above her breast throb. "Tell me."

"Suprasternal notch!"

"That's right," she said. "You want to touch it. Flick out your tongue, baby, and slip me that code."

"I remember!"

And he stood bolt upright, knocking the chair back on its wheels. The door crashed open and agents in black vests and BDUs stormed in. Stormed in like lightning and rain and wailing wind for all the shouting and waving guns and clanking belts and squeaking boots.

"Wait a minute!"

The men ranged round him with poised barrels. He unbuckled and dropped his pants. Of course he went commando. He worked from home, after all. And there standing bold as a big leaguer's bat was his pulsing pink member. And, man, was his dick embarrassed. However, the agents remained unfazed. Stalwart and deadly and clad in uniforms snug enough to keep genitalia neatly in place. They inched forward and Richard felt every inch of his skin prickle with fear.

"Hold!" Anassas said. "Hold your men, commander."

Richard's arms up and his meat flouncing. A man in black slowly lowered his rifle. Looked Richard square in the eyes before dropping the gaze in a squint. He came back quick with an arm up and clenched fist.

"Hold!" he said.

The only word he said. Because he's not a main character so he doesn't require further lines. But Anassas is and she does. So she leaned in even closer, if you can imagine it, and squinted herself. Looking directly at where Richard's penis was. Or would have been if he'd turn to her. So she said:

"Turn to me."

And he did.

"Bring your dick up here."

And he pushed forward.

"Hold it back so I can see."

And he pushed the tip against his belly. She picked up a pen and started writing frantically. She stood up and handed the paper to a person on approach.

"Send this to Control."

The person glanced at Richard and his pinned shaft and spun out of the room.

"I thought you said we were alone," Richard said.

She sat back in her chair, waved a hand and said:

"It's a bit late for that now, don't you think?"

Richard turned his head and noticed that all the muzzles had been lowered. He returned to the screen where the entire rectangle was honeyed waves over milky skin to pursed pink lips that almost ached to touch the shuddering shaft between his fingers. At least Richard hoped the ache was real. She was smiling and those stony greens softened enough to let light swim lazy and carefree in the irises. Trapped like angels in a twinned-heaven.

"You've saved the world," she said. "You've saved all of us."

"Oh, it was nothing," he said.

She pointed a finger and licked her lips. Richard would swear that she did. He didn't care if there were people behind him. They could be witnesses to the love growing between them. Or lust. I mean, Richard would be fine if it were just lust. Still pointing she said:

"I wouldn't say that was nothing."

And so he looked down for the first time and saw letters and numbers written on the underside of his stuck-up stinger. He was about to ask how the hell they got there, but he was so dreadfully tired of regretting things said to the goddess shimmering through the screen. And his shift still hadn't officially started.

"Klaxon Corp. will be forever indebted to you,"

Anassas said.

"Well, shit," he said.

And hardly regretted that statement since it brought a smile to those queenly lips and made an angel laugh. And when angels laugh it's like being kissed all over. Right up to the tippy-top of your extended being.

Newborn Baby Has Lazy Eye

This is for Sage because this is about Sage.

Sage Richmond isn't dead, but maybe he wishes he were.

Now. But it's not now. It's then.

Unemployed and whiling away his late mornings and early afternoons before the glowing monitor. Chats and posts and memes interchangeable and incessant. Bouncing around like a bunny in a big pile of cocaine. Chicanery afoot, or more appropriately, a finger as Sage the Rabbit hops it from one tab to another, screen to screen, program to program, tips of fingers ceaselessly flickering over the board for fingers, endlessly flying from image on a springboard fashioned from his imagination. Fashioned, erected, scaled and declaiming by megaphone the fruits of his tireless efforts. Tireless between 10AM and 3PM. A matchless warrior in the swing shift hours. Otherwise, fuck that shit. Sage wasn't about to get up early for anyone. Or work into the evening for that matter. The Muse would have to await his resurrection from the unburned bed, stumbling to the resuscitated computer with that life-giving tip of finger, plopping himself to pleather with a sigh because he'd forgotten to put on the coffee. And so now the Muse would have to wait even longer for Sage Ramses to return with a miniature cauldron steaming with the roil of water of bean. Or bean of water. Where have you been, Sage? Where have you bean? No answer. Whatever, Muse, think on that.

A photoshopped epiphany like a bolt of lightning. Luminescent fuzz from the screen. A sip of bean water and the thoughts colliding within the hallowed chamber of his head. Some old-world photo of a man suffering from pellagra. That pain being neatly decapitated. Another picture of a cousin of Sage who Sage knew to be an asshole. Very nearly truly with a wispy mustache the color of poop and thickness of taint hair. Breath of compost left in the sun. So thankfully, gratefully snicked the head from that poor lesioned soul and replaced with that straight on gaping bunghole of a cousin. Neatly, wondrously stitched together in poetic justice. Frankenstein's monster unleashed upon his friends, to the public as the button for the book of face was selected. Selected by Sage the Manipulator to wreak his revenge upon those who'd wronged him or that he'd wronged and hated or that he hated himself for doing but couldn't stop himself anyway. And the Muse tipped its hat because it wears a hat for that express purpose when those who it inspires performs a task worthy of the finger flip.

"Shazing," Sage said, firing a double-barreled handgun at the screen. "You always were a pud."

Next up on deck of the ball of base. A friend with whom he'd lost touch. Since the school was high. Not a falling out so much as a drifting apart. He couldn't remember why. But he trolled for the right pose and was blessed by the Muse with a wet smack of lips on his head foremost. Stock photo of a child with rickets: bow-legged and arms twisting out of frame. The tool of snicking applied and another head to hover in bloodless space. Reattached to a new host body. No more bones buckle under pressure. No more fractured steps fraught with dissolution from that black-and-white child blown around by that bowl of dust. Sage the Mercy Killer. A young, undoctored Kevorkian with the fingers to resurrect any human or conglomeration of humans or unidentifiable Sage-spawn unleashed upon the masses. That high school friend of a yesteryear with hair flowing out of frame just like the arms to the ricketted body sent swiftly on wings into the space of cyber. Cyberhellacious and hellishly, hilariously sent to fumble through that new world on crutches.

"Shazing." Two guns out firing this time. "You weren't that interesting anyway."

Another hot gulp of bean water. A loud sigh and moment's reflection. Who next? Who next, Sage? And no one answered since no one had spoken. Sage closed his eyes and leaned back, tapping tips of fingers on the desk before the board of keys. Jangling through his brain those images from which to pick. As if stainless steel or nickel alloy or whatever keys are made from. Ringing in a chorus from the breath of the Muse. Wind chimes and black empty space before a nascent image came straight to the fore. Straight on and gaping but not an asshole, like the cousin. The picture of innocence and toothless joy. Happily, beatifically drooling down its baby chin. The infant of the What's-their-names. That weird couple who always wore black. Harry, maybe. What was her name, Sage? But no one answered again because, like before, no one had spoken. And so the Muse brushed his cortex at the front with lashes grown of softest silk. Abigail. That was it. But did he have a picture of the baby? Do you know, Jamie? [Of course he has a picture of the baby. Duh. *Ed.*] In any case, someone must know, else the story couldn't continue. And the Muse kept batting its invisible lashes.

"The shazing must continue," Sage said. "Even if it's the innocent. No one shall be spared the sting of Sir Sage's cyber wit."

No one indeed, Sir Sage, though you've never been knighted. You have to have a job for that. Be employed by a king or queen. And Sage had been unemployed by a far less aristocratic body of corporate.

"What about the shazing?" But Sage had only repeated the words of the Muse.

He stumbled upon a picture of that grinning baby.

Eyes wide open and staring. Shine from drool and nearly hairless. Wisps of blond but lashes the darkness of Satan's heart. If Satan had a heart. Distended round those baby blues like guard hair. The look of wonder right before it gives way to resolution. The physiognomy never seen on a face so young. Yet, there sat that very expression. And Sage couldn't pass up such a propitious gift sent tightly, snuggly packaged by the Muse.

"Holy mother of God," Sage said. "I've hit the mother lode."

And that vein of precious metal bit into and locked. Set to screen and rummaging the trash bin, storage space, umpteen sources of inspiration laid out like dominoes on the two-dimensional floor of the net intertwined within. Which surrogate body would bring the biggest laugh? The greatest satisfaction? Sage scratched his head right where the Muse kept kicking him. But it wasn't coming through. The images seemed vacuous and sun-damaged compared with the brilliantly, knowingly upturned face of the baby. He flickered through and nattered to himself since no one was there to hear him except the Muse. And apparently, disappointingly the Muse was deaf.

"Come on, Musey Muse," Sage said. "Bring me the shazing."

But the Muse wasn't someone to be ordered about because the Muse was precisely no one at all. Only a figment of Sage the Distorter's febrile mind. Well, not fevered exactly. It could have just been the coffee. For strong stuff it was. Stronger than mere water passed over or squeezed out of beans. It had the point of fire-tempered steel affixed to a spear. And his tips of fingers couldn't type fast enough. Function keys tripping over themselves in the race to bring the bright new thing to life. The idea. The idea! He had it and it resonated in the very hairs stuck up round the baby's blazing eyes. The Muse just stood on and watched. Shuffling in a corner. Sadly, impotently humming a tune that wasn't really a tune since there really wasn't anyone there to hum it. And so now Sage began to hum. And smile. And his eyes softened before the image he'd created out of dust, blowing life through the nostrils, forming a body from a rib of the Muse since she didn't need it anyway.

"Oh, my dear Lord," said Sage the Blasphemer. "That's the funniest shit I've ever seen."

And for him it was true. Wholeheartedly, depressingly so. He leaned back and soaked it in, through the pores. An osmotic humor of humours that changed the very chemistry behind the muscles to his flabby, underworked face. For there before him sat that same drooling infant with those same precocious eyes. Except that one of them had wandered. The pupil staring out of frame, maybe catching a glance at rickets-twisted limbs. And not horrified, that truant eye. The same sense of pre-resolution to all horror of life and life in horror and the horrifying unrealities of supernatural existence. That blue iris bent at an angle made Sage weep with hilarity. And pity. A mix, really, honestly, because there was something so sad and yet so funny about a baby with a lazy eye. And that image concocted by the laziest of them all. Sage the Lord of Lackadaisicalia.

"Shazing!" And you already know Sage said it. "Bless my fucking stars."

And then there was a rap at the door. And it definitely wasn't the Muse since it was in Sage's head. But not really. Yet shuffling and definitely not knocking or anything. She had even stopped humming since the rapping on the door made her look up. At what exactly no one can say since no one can say what nothing can see with any real degree of accuracy. Point hammered home, so up and at 'em with a mug o' joe.

So Sage opened the door. He'll wish he hadn't. But that's now, not then, and who cares what Sage thinks now anyway? Surely not the Muse. She flew the coop of Sage's head for less turbulent and fouled space. What a clutter the attic of that man, am I right, Jamie? [Yes! Absolutely. *Ed.*]

"Holy shit," Sage said.

Because Harry and what's-her-name, Abigail, were there. Holding a baby. The baby. The one without the lazy eye and all the experience of a millennia's-old demon behind it.

"Hello," the man said.

Sage nodded. Still dumbfounded but maybe more actually annoyed at the disturbance.

"Sage, right," the man said. "Sage Richmond?"

"Well, if I were a rich man I wouldn't have to work hard," Sage said. "In fact, I'm not currently working at all."

He stood straighter. As if proud of the fact. Sage wasn't one of those hamsters spinning wheels. He wasn't locked in an office with jailhouse food pushed on a tray through a slot in the door. He had the Muse to guide him. Well, actually, she'd flown that barnyard of a brain. So then bereft and yet in pajamas. He was no wheel-spinning rodent. No figment of his or anyone else's imagination was going to make him run in circles. He had his own genius.

"Yes, well," the woman holding the baby said. "The Harrisons recommended you."

"The Harrisons?"

"The folks at the end of the street," the man said. "At the corner of the intersection."

"You mean where that crazy recluse used to live?" Sage said. "The guy who yelled from his porch."

"No," the woman said. "The house diagonal from that." And when that failed to jog recall: "The house with all the pretty purple flowers."

"And the trees," the man said.

"Oh," Sage said. "You mean the Scatterings."

"The Harrisons."

"The Scatterings."

The man shrugged and the woman shrugged so

Sage shrugged as well. But the baby remained still. It stared at Sage with the expression of a brain surgeon who knows just exactly what the inside of a human head looks like. And it was drooling. The river Styx down the chin and soaking into its Onesies.

"We were wondering," the woman said, "if you'd be available to watch little Eshy tonight while we go to our . . . meeting."

"Yes, it's very important," the man said.

Sage rubbed that sore spot from where he'd been kicked by the Muse. And the baby bore its cobalt drills into bone. Maybe trying to find that soft spot. But babies were supposed to be the ones with the soft spots. What was the name of that, Sage?

Fontanel.

And the baby bore right into him still. Drooling. And maybe that word had slipped from those blubbering lips. And Sage never had a soft spot for babies. And the baby seemed to know it.

"Eshy?"

"Eshmun, actually," the man said. "He's named for an ancient god."

"A weak god," the woman said.

"Not all that weak," the man said turning to her. "Just . . . conflicted."

"Nobody will miss him," she said.

There was silence. That silence filled the void. And that void matched the same void in Sage's head. The baby kept staring at him while the parents looked down. And now a word grew in his head. And he had no idea why it was there but he knew who put it there. It was the baby and its eyes were blazingly, smirkingly open. MOLOCH filled his braincase. And he hoped he was spelling it right, because it was more felt than seen, that word.

"You want me to babysit?" Sage said.

"Oh, would you?" the woman said. "That would

be ever so kind."

"But I don't even know your names."

But he did. Or at least thought he did, Sage the Liar. But he wanted to hear them say it. To say anything to drown out that pagan god from his skull. MOLOCH. What an absurdity. Sure, he didn't exactly like kids. Give 'em lazy eyes and such and push that shit out on the internet. But he didn't require sacrifices of them. Didn't want them dead. Just taken away so someone else could change the diapers.

"Harry," the man said, extending his hand.

Tall. Short hair. Severe face. Like the edge of an axe facing you. Or Sage, rather, because you're not there. And be glad you're not. Just ask Jamie. [Clearly the baby is going to murder Sage in his sleep. *Ed.*]

"Abigail," the woman said, nodding.

Red waves. Milk white flesh. Plump lips. The face of a murderer after it convinced everyone that she hadn't committed murder.

And why so long for the descriptions? Maybe Sage hadn't really noticed them since he was so preoccupied with the baby. Or maybe was just lazy. Well, that for sure is the truth. But no amount of procrastination could deflect the cutting depth of those baby blues.

"So," Abigail said. "Do you think you could watch Eshy for a couple of hours?"

"We'd pay you well," Harry said.

Hey Dad, the baby said in Sage's head. You already paid.

Hadad?

Sage shook his noggin to stop it from going numb.

"How much?" he said.

"More than enough," Abigail said.

Ask her, huh, the baby said. There's no depth they won't go to.

Asherah?

Sage's face felt tingly and it wasn't from the cold

100

air because it wasn't cold outside.

"It'd have to be," Sage said. "I'm pretty busy."

"We understand," Abigail said. "And we wouldn't bother you if it weren't for this . . ."

"Meeting," Harry said.

"Yes, you said."

"So, what do you say?"

What do you say, Sage? You'll shit your pants now or you'll do it later. Either way, it's all going to catch up with you. They'll all catch up with you. It's easy to sneak up on someone when they never move. Slack-muscled prey in a cave. And who were they? Molochstation. Infestation. If he let this weirdness in anything could slip through. And then where would he be? He couldn't be rude. Sage the Attaché to pagan gods.

Man, fuck those gods. Fuck those gods in the ear.

"I can't say no to that cute face," Sage said, holding out his arms. "Come here, little Eshy."

Don't you think this conversation's gone on long enough? the baby said in Sage's head when he grabbed him and held him to his chest. And at his chest the tiny head nestled, still staring up into Sage's face. I'll eat your heart, Sage knew it said. And he felt a faint thumping at the top of his belly. Like there'd been a fetus with a heartbeat in his womb. But of course Sage didn't have a womb. He was man of woman born, after all. But nonetheless, something had been conceived within him. And not even when the Muse had left him had he felt so alone. Alone and with an evil forming limbs from a goopy mass. That heartbeat beneath his own flesh matching the baby's own faint flutters. And the eyes seemed to pulse, almost. The irises shutter slightly, singularly as if rocked by approaching earthquakes.

"Thank you," Harry and Abigail had said.

But they had left him, too. Probably with instructions. Some list, at least, for taking proper care of the offspring of Satan. And sprung off on him like some ticking bomb and he the vacant car. Some malevolence metastasizing in his never-worked belly. So he held the baby away from his own body as if the separation would rip out that demon seed. He went inside and closed the door on the outside world that held diminutive gods by comparison. Maybe Eshy was only a baby, but it instilled a great big fear in the corpulent heart of Sage the Doomed. So he put the baby on the couch and watched it stare up at him. Again. Never looking away for an instant. Those circular saws of blue biting into his corneas and making him weep. Weep for humanity! Weep for the fallen! Weep, for Jesus' sake, weep until that river washes you straight out of that hell. Ride the back of Acheron into the dazzling wash of the sun in the cool blue sky. Blue. Like the eyes. Biting and biting and ripping through rock. Deep enough to set in a bolt. And hang a picture of the hosts of Hell laughing and pointing at Sage the Damned on red hot pikes and lifted to the sky. Blue. Like the tongues of demons sticking out and mocking. Spitting fire because that's what devils do. Helplessly, hopelessly flailing on the sharpened staff. Sage the Impaled and hailed by the demon horde as the last human left to torture. And the last image to see are those spinning, chugging, ripping baby blues. Blue. And Sage blew it he knew. It was too late.

"What the hell are you looking at?" he said to the baby.

And in his head he heard back the ring of Hell! Hell! Hell!

"Jesus Christ, you're freaking me out, kid."

You flabby freak of nature, in his head. And what baby talks like that anyway? Lucifer's baby, that's who. Or so it does in the overactive imagination of Sage the Truth Slayer.

"Oh good fucking God in Heaven."

This blasphemy brought to you by the letter F. F for Fear. F for Freak of nature. F for Fuck this shit. And that was Sage all over. Screw that noise and blow this joint. Leave the baby to F for Fend for itself on the plush couch. Plush enough for a rocking cataclysm to widen those cushions and swallow the baby whole. Sucked back into the hellwomb from which it had gestated. Fiendishly, frighteningly choking that baby down a couch-sized gullet and squeezing it home. Shat out on a steaming pile. Whether fecal matter or coals or human remains turned to carbon. But those eyes, those ever-gnawing eyes.

And now one eye had drifted. A moon knocked out of orbit into perpetual night. Dark side of the lazy eye!

Sage squeaked like a stepped-on puppy and backed into the coffee table. he fell and backpedaled his ass to the far wall. The baby sputtering and spitting all down itself. Some primordial ointment as offering to whichever hellbeings held sway in Sage's living room. Now that the baby had been brought in. Now that its eye had drifted. Now that it clumsily, soundlessly clapped its chubby hands together.

I bet you'll taste good with all that fat, the baby said in his head.

Sage screamed and jumped up. He bolted through the doorway, catching the lintel with a shoulder, spiraling into the hallway and crashing into paneling. A mirror shook on the wall. In the corner he could see the baby still slapping its arms. But the eye had righted. The eye had righted! Maybe just a trick in reverse. But he dared not look back. So he stepped closer to the glass and looked deep within. And found himself staring back. The right eye slipping even further to the right. Drifted and damned like that planetless moon. He screamed one more time and shook in a dengue fever fit. He shook and gasped like a man a moment before expiring on the deathbed.

"Shazing," he said.

The baby giggled as he hit the floor.

Arts of Darkness

From the darkness crept the man and the darkness clung to him like a cloak. Coal black fingers in latex and torpedo gripped gently enough to sense the pulsing artery of his quarry. Oil-slick slinks into soft fluorescents at the back of the room at the end of the hall. Shark tooth grip with fin flights in foil. Steel tip coated in the blood of Blue Rocket. Iridescent finish and painstaking stalking down the corridor. Ever closer to that warm glow. Steps and then halting in the center of frame. Within that frame a red burning tip. An exhale of smoke that dissipates into the unflickering bulbs overhead. And unflinching that patient predator on unsqueaking feet.

Aim: eyes, dart and target in one line.

Backword move: slow and far back as possible.

Acceleration: not too fast or with too much force. Wrist snap while hand goes forward.

Release: should happen naturally.

Follow-through: hand should end up aiming at target.

Or so the experts say.

And before the man can turn around, lit cig in fingers and tense, the projectile is on its way, point slowly up and leveling out, a parabolic flight unheard and unseen, and that already corded neck tingling before impact. The man drops the cigarette and slaps at a damaged vessel. Another flung missile and another. Tight grouping. Tiny thuds like winged fowl as they hit the ground. A shaking and collapsing against the walls and the fluorescents bleed unaltered. A fist manages to rip one dart from flesh and spurts fly chiaroscuro. The black-clad predator dips back into darkness and allows only the eyes to reflect the dark deed perpetrated mere feet away. And that crumpled man shakes and pulls at a collar and kicks out at nothing as blood drains into the carpet below. Shuddering like those birds before the jaws of the hunting dogs close around brittle ribs. Shattered wings. The man closes his eyes and the attacker stands again and steps forward. Into the warm yet friendless glow. Silent black shifting through molecules in air that stir and stick like burs on the dogs' coats. He bends and extracts the two darts once all motion has stilled. All breath dissipated like that puff of smoke from the last cigarette this man would ever smoke. And where there's smoke there's a killer who set the fire. Searching eyes find the third dart at the twitchless feet. Nimble fingers open a case buckled to his belt and all three murdering missiles are deposited inside, the crack of jaws meeting as the lid snaps shut. Latex gloves rolled, turned inside out and pocketed. Uncracking joints as he pushes away into that deepening gloom. A dissolution into the interminable dark corridor.

And as the experts say.

Follow-through: one continuous motion upon completion of the contract.

Release: let it go. Forget about it.

Acceleration: unhurried flight before witnesses show.

Backward move: a shrug then head down.

Aim: for the exit door and the hell out of there.

Arc of darkness. And the still breath of the dead of night.

"Cole?"
"Yes."

"We need to speak."

"We already are."

Dead air.

"You didn't finalize the deal."

"Seemed pretty final to me."

"You didn't leave the message."

"There was no message."

"The card."

"You mean the advertisement?"

"You know what I mean."

"I'm not a shill."

"You were given a task."

"What I do is an art. Leaving the message would've been artless. It would've cheapened the whole thing."

"You were paid."

"And now one less obstacle is in your way."

"Not in mine."

"You know what I mean."

Silence that bled into the phantom distance between the voices.

"They'll be coming for you."

"Let them."

"Cole, these guys aren't the type you fuck with."

"Easy now, this line could be recorded."

"I'm serious."

"And so was I. Let them come."

"Why couldn't you have just left the card?"

"Because I'm not a salesman, like I said. Flytes can get some other sucker."

"Flytes is just the front."

"OK. I'm biting."

"Klaxon Corp.'s the wolf."

"Oh, shit."

"And they have a long memory."

"And now I know this line is definitely not being recorded."

A quiet tickling at the neck just below the ear.
"You were the best, Cole."
"It's not over yet."
"Yes it is."

A pounding at the door. Why do they always announce themselves like this? So tacky, Cole knows, just like he knows that in seconds they'll come crashing through with a battering ram since that's the best solution these flat-headed bounders could bang together. But he'd been ready for them. All bulbs unscrewed and their smashed bodies strewn about the room. Sure they'll be wearing boots with soles thicker than tank tread. And he'll hear every crushing step.

Aim: for the first sorry bastard who bursts through the door.

Backward move: holding out to the last possible instant.

Acceleration: a piercing scream along the tip.

Release: into the ebon arms of night.

Follow-through: finger pointing at the glinting foil fin pointing back.

More deadly glints as mounted spotlights hit arrows midair. And those pointed beams falling forward and canting upward as the necks of the intruders are struck. Frail pigeon bones break under foot and knee and shoulder as the herd falls one by one. Fall down, fall back, fall forward, fall all around as bullets spray in disarray. And the spray from punctured arteries. Heavy muscle colliding and spiraling. Grunts and screams in the dark. A whisking through black-jacketed bodies. Bolts in meat sent in spasms. And the dart of arcness, over and over, sailing amongst the scattered, the broken army in the field. And Cole sailing, too, through the very air almost, jamming home points in carotids and eyes and temples and slipping right back out of range. Pouring on hell, raining down death. Arrows to blot out the sun if there had been a sun to illuminate the distorted faces of the fallen, the bleeding, the bleating, the brash braggadocio of pumped up he-men crushed into a flailing, many-armed, lumpy ball.

Aim: automatic fire tearing up the plaster.

Backward move: squeezing between bodies out the door.

Acceleration: flat-out running down the stairwell.

Release: the back exit door blown open.

Follow-through: diving through the hedges and disintegrating into memory.

But the wolf did have a long memory. So disintegration or otherwise wouldn't help. The wolf would reintegrate all those infinitesimal pieces and put together the man who had set the trap and taken its foot. And the wolf was done licking its wounds. Some lupine Hephaestus had fashioned a new, better, stronger leg. And that powerful limb itched with the memory that could never be forgotten.

"Who is this?"
"You have to ask?"
"I just did."
"Then you're already dead."
"Then how am I speaking?"
"You're a ghost of yourself."
"And you sound like a ghost, too, over the phone."
"And this voice will be the last one you ever hear."
"Why, are you leaving?"
"No, you are."
"I'm not going anywhere because I'm not anywhere."

111

"Waxing philosophical will not prevent your death."

"And death won't stop philosophy."

"You think you're smart, don't you?"

"I only need to be smarter than you."

"But you aren't, Cole. You're so dreadfully shortsighted."

"I'm still alive."

"You're a ghost, like I've said."

"Then stop repeating yourself."

A chuckle.

"OK, then. You're smart. Just as smart as the fox that's caught by the hunter."

"I thought this was supposed to be funny."

"What do you mean?"

"Well, it's just that everything that's preceded this had some element of humor. This is just gloomy and absurd."

"Some people think absurdity is funny."

"Some people."

"I think this is a laugh riot."

"Do go on."

"You don't think this is funny?"

"I will when you call me after having failed yet again to kill me."

A ghostly chuckle again. But the threat was anything but apparition. It was all meat. Red, dripping meat.

"Have you heard the one about the surgeon whose scalpel slipped while performing endarterectomy?"

"OK. I'm biting."

"He got carotid away."

Just how it was that Flytes, a dartboard manufacturer of middling renown, happened to be acquired by or be the front for or had turned into the big slobbering dog of a company, namely Klaxon Corp., is a fact that Cole would never hold between his black-industrial latex-stretched fingers. The last thing held between those fingers would be the talking end of a payphone. And why a payphone? Because it's funnier. I mean, who uses those things nowadays? In any case, the reason that that outmoded piece of telecommunication had been the final object he held was because of the dart sticking out of his throat. From out of nowhere and hitting nothing vital, exactly, just smarting like hell. But then two more missiles had hit appropriately home just as he'd dropped the receiver and just had time to turn toward his assailant. Of course, he couldn't see him for he was nowhere to be seen. Just as Cole had thought he wasn't anywhere, so had his attacker. Well, his murderer, really, because Cole as sure as shit is going to die. Just look at those wide eyes, hands to neck, slumped against the carpet in a corridor that seemed all too familiar. He couldn't hear the killer on approach since he could only hear laughter from the phone swinging on its cord.

Carotid away. Cole had to admit that was pretty good.

Aim: a being emerges from the darkness.

Backward move: a hand glides inside a jacket pocket.

Acceleration: a piece of paper flicked with the wrist.

Release: flutters to the floor at the forehead.

Follow-through: bending at the knees and leaning in.

"Regards of Klaxon Corp.," the man says.

And just before his blood can obliterate the name, Flytes in party font taunts from a bone-white business card. The man stands and retreats into a world grown ever darker. And Cole just blinks at the fluorescents like a ghost would just before exhaling and joining all other wispy non-entities in the ether.

"I told you it would be funny, Cole."

"Yeah, hilarious."

"Come on, where's your sense of humor?"

"Bleeding into cheap carpet."

"Don't be so negative."

"But it's more irony than humor, isn't it?"

"Some people think irony is really funny."

"Some people."

"Well, have you heard the one about the guy who went to see a chiropractor and was asked the same question over and over?"

"Man, you know, you're a real pain in the neck."

"So you have heard it."

On the Mend

"Give me some fishing line and I'll stitch myself in time."

So Orpheus had said.

Not the god of classical antiquity. But the modern man falling apart in his own bedroom. Literally falling apart. And from the medical supply store he'd bought catgut suture or more likely suture thread formed from synthetic polymer fibers. But catgut's more evocative so we'll stick with that. Stick, ha! because he'd gotten some needles, too. Well, actually they all came together as a set since the ends of the needles were swaged. In any case, round-bodied stainless steel in a C-curve with atraumatic suture. It better be atraumatic since it's going to hurt like the Devil's red peter in the back side. ⅜ circle should do it, he knew, since he'd watched enough YouTube videos on how to stitch flesh back together again—wounds, severed digits, organs, the softest of tissues. He was ready and he'd taken a shot of whiskey even though he hated whiskey. The ragged line running just above his elbow and snaking its way into the hollow. He squeezed the tear together and pinched the needle two-thirds back from the point. He closed his eyes and sat as still as a patient during examination. Until forced to cough. But he wasn't coughing. A sharp intake. Holding it. A deep release.

"For every gash a loss and every scar a victory."

So Orpheus said.

Eyes opened to piercing reality. He threaded the needle through damaged meat, tongue stuck out to the left. Jabbing fire and now he wished he'd taken another swig of that detestable whiskey. Ants red and flaming following the curve below the bicep. Sweat beaded on the forehead like jewels in a diadem. But he was no Greek god, so make no mistake about the sweat. It was all very human. And though he happened to be sitting on the edge of his bed, he wasn't resting, he was working — and working hard. So no one could accuse him of being lazy. Or of hubris. And just when he'd neatly snipped the line and placed the scissors to the worn padding of his comforter, another tear caused his right arm to swing in an arc and fall to the floor. How in the world was he going to manage that reattachment with one arm? Oh how Orpheus wished he were a god! Then he'd understand his ignominious fate. And the Fates were gods, too. But no one was assailing him. And he had no godlike powers. So like a good and proper human should, he bent over and retrieved his limb from the floor.

"Leaves fall at their appointed time as fresh green shoots burst in theirs."

Orpheus said.

The palm to the disconnected arm was placed against one of the columns to his four-poster bed. Not one of those big fancy ones the regents had during the reign of the House of Bourbon. Tubular and hollow so that when the hand slipped, a knuckle rapped on the post and rang out in false splendor. Bourbon. That reminded him that he wanted to down more whiskey to quell the pain, even if its burn flipped the stomach. But it could wait. It would have to wait. He'd only one arm, after all! So back up again, caught in the notch between thumb and forefinger, and gritting teeth as he fought to align it to his shoulder. This was going to be difficult, he knew. And it would probably be crooked later. Oh well, no use in crying over spilt limbs. He needed to see clearly in any case. The sweat was hard enough to keep from vision, brushing his other arm across his brow. And across the bow a warning shot fired as the hand slipped again and knuckled black metal. Back in place, notched like an arrow, alignment as good as could be expected under the circumstances. Needle up and in and out and in and out and in and out as the fire ants danced in tortured rhythm. Another slip but enough stitches to catch the arm from thudding to the floorboards. Like a damaged wing it hung. And like a maddened scientist drunk on laudanum and discovery he continued his surgery until those jewels in his crown crashed to his chest with the thunder of triumph just behind. With a sigh he rotated the reattached branch and felt the bark buckle and crack. It wasn't perfect. Couldn't quite feel the tips of each finger. And there was a buzzing line around the shoulder as if he'd swallowed a tiny sewing machine. A sewing machine! Man, how he'd sing for one of those sewers. But for now he'd have to settle for his own inexpert yet informed handiwork. He sighed and went to stand and instead found himself flat on his back on the floor. The left leg had torn free at the knee and it was all he could do, poor Orpheus, to fling himself off his wings. But of course he didn't have wings. He wasn't a bug. Just felt like one. The sort of beetle cruel children hold up to the sun as they pull off all the legs. Did I fail to mention that his last name was Cicone? A bit of irony there, too, or fate, or Fates, or what-have-you. Nonetheless, the toes from his left foot twitched to right itself.

"Stout legs on which to stand or else knees to fall upon and die."

Orpheus.

Up from the floor and onto the bed. His pajamas furled past shredded tendon at the knee. At least he'd had both arms to contend with now. Two arms against the endless crumbling of his body. Tongue out and to the left again as he lined it up, bit in deep with the point, rolling in loops from hand to hand and circumnavigating twice just to make sure it was secure. It was a leg, after all. The pant leg unfurled and he stood to test the stitches. They creaked as much as the floorboards, but remained intact. Held firm. Like his resolve to put himself back together. Maybe not the prettiest creature on God's green planet, but alive and mobile and holding steady. Well, maybe not God, but evolution. Whatever it was that set this slow slide into disassembly. Whatever law of nature or act of God. Whatever curse or fate or destiny. Whichever being or force to curse the fate he'd been destined. And he was beyond all that, anyhow, since he'd stitched order back into place. He'd bitten past the pain and into the freedom of four working limbs. He'd wrested chaos from whoever's fists had tried to rip him into irreparable dissolution. He'd upended those malign spirits and tossed them into the yawning void. Both feet firmly planted and going nowhere without the rest of the body to follow.

"I think I have to sneeze."

So Orpheus said before he actually did and blew the right leg clean off.

"Will there be no end or will the end be the end of me?"

He shrugged but then checked himself. The left ear felt wiggly and Orpheus knew it was just a matter of time before that, too, dropped like hail from an indifferent sky. Well, the indifferent plaster really, since he was in his bedroom, after all. So he held his ear and hopped into the room where the bottle of whiskey and a shot glass waited on a table.

"This is going to be a long night, Orpheus."

Said.

Holystoning

Dr. Karkur suffered the strangest dreams. One dream, really, broken into shards and reassembled, piece by piece, every night with acrylic polymer into a salvageable whole. An artifact of distinction.

Before the dreams there had been stories from a Malay guide. Some too fantastic to believe, some too tantalizing to outright dismiss. And each tale told with unwavering delivery. Each had its special place and its special significance in the man's mythos. But each had equal power — equal sanctity. Except for one. The guide shook and looked over both shoulders before relating this singular bit of dark history.

"Dark, dark days," the guide had said.

As if he'd been there. But of course he hadn't. The setting was centuries old. Yet, maybe the ooze from some primordial deep had long since mixed with the blood of the native population. And maybe, too, if you'd cut this man's flesh — severed a vein — that black ichor would seep into the floor of the jungle and sizzle like steam off a roasted skull. And why a roasted skull? Well, those are just the kind of images conjured in the mind of the good doctor by the guide's story. And the shaking man had looked over both shoulders again.

Apparently, some Dutch sailing vessel had drifted outside the range of its proper kingdom, dissolving into fog, hiding in coves, disappearing into heat waves along the horizon. This ship was of the republic, but not in the republic of the Dutch any longer, being more properly the reflection of the rotten dead heart of the colonizers, set on the unattainable periphery to mock those on the shores and in the boats still piloted by humans. For the guide had said this outlier was inhabited by demons, or at the least, that the humans had been possessed by those demons. And those demons fed on blood and pain and wailing and the brutal crush of mortals into the groaning planks. And that blood was never enough. The demons were ever thirsty, ever watchful of stray passengers on stray vessels spanking through the waters to inevitable doom. Great holystones were brought to the deck, the guide said, to scour blood from the boards, collecting the gore in buckets and tossing them over the gunwales. And the chanting! The guide's head twisted all about when mentioning the chanting. As if there were voices in his head and the only reason they were there was because the black ooze was in his blood and that blood fed his brain. Maybe the fish all up and down the Malacca Strait had swum in that blood, had drunk that blood, for so long that it became part of them, too. And the natives had caught and feasted on their flesh, thereby ingesting the black ooze. Then just a matter of time before the whole shoreline, the whole island up to the mountains, was just as blank and cursed and perpetually unsated as the demons on board that woeful vessel of centuries ago.

Or so the guide had said. And this is where Dr. Karkur had to stop him. He didn't come here for this incessant blubbering gibberish. He came to study the Kantoli and Sri Vijaya kingdoms. The artifacts. biofacts and architecture. Cultural landscapes. Not a mishmash of selective history from the mouth of a man too scared to not keep glancing backward.

"Yes, I'm sure they were dark days," the doctor had said. "But where did you say you found the unusual stones?"

The first part of the dream had come to him upon his first night's sleep back in the States. Hands grabbed at him in the darkness. Stilted voices and pushing him forward. In protest, he opened his mouth and yelled, and was immediately smashed in the face with a cudgel. He fell to his knees and felt a tooth barely hanging on by torn tissue. Couldn't help tonguing the miniature disaster as those same hands grabbed and hauled him to his feet. Wobbly and near insensate and rushed down the length of the ship. He didn't know where he was. What part of the ship. What part of the world. Only that the voices spoke a language unfamiliar to him. He bled from the mouth and at least took comfort in the damage. Some kind of anchor. But where were they taking him? And why were they laughing? And why as no one trying to help him?

He didn't tell anyone about the dream, at least that initial glimpse of it, because he never bothered anyone with any of his dreams. Not that he'd ever had much occasion to. Dreamless and preoccupied and satisfactorily fulfilled in his endeavors. Even at the research lab at university, sitting beside Dr. Sparfield, scraping rust from a metal artifact with a dental pick, he hadn't bothered to mention it. The dream was engulfed by the smoke of memory, by the hum of the AC fans. Forgotten like a people subsumed by another more dangerous people. Lost in shadows of jungle regrowth.

"Have you taken a look at the stones yet?" the doctor had said.

Dr. Sparfield hadn't troubled to turn her head. "Yeah, just sandstone blocks."

"Holystones."

"Come again?"

"They used them on ships to scour the decks."

Dr. Sparfield shrugged her shoulders. Dr. Karkur noted how she hadn't found the need to look back both ways. The horror of centuries ago, or the confabulation of those horrors, had become unmoored and drifted somewhere in the South Pacific. Lost to him. Never discovered by her. The point of the pick digging at an ancient feature.

"Surprised they survived, they're so brittle," she'd said.

Dr. Karkur had followed the guide through the phantasmagoria of the South Sumatran jungle: Eocene flowers, giant fronds ever-shifting in the wind, rust-colored trunks to trees battling far above, an orangutan, maybe, and more stories of tigers and crocodiles taking unwary trespassers into darkened dens and dank pools, and the egrets that wing over plains of human bones, the trunks of those pines fissured like the scarified survivors of the horrors ensuring that those stories would be forever reiterated. And the jungle would always remain a dream. The mist in the distance off a green-choked incline through the clutching aperture they'd approached would soon infuse their skin with its wafting violence. Impressionable visions. The smoke from narcotics off a great funeral pyre. But it could have just been the stories.

The good doctor shook himself and marched through that hole torn into the otherworldly canopy. Good, because he'd not thought it otherworldly, just evidence of evolution vying for its place in the sun amongst all the other clawing, scratching, rending creatures. Good, because he didn't believe in the evil and never allowed it a foothold in how he treated those who served him. Good, because he knew they weren't servants. Not even the guide. Just a man making do like every other human on this rolling, sprouting, living, dying planet. Good, too, because the doctor believed he could make a difference. And that difference was the discovery to who we had been. Yes, we, because he put himself squarely among all those other humans who had to claw and scratch to get themselves anywhere further down the road of a better existence. Except that he used picks and mattocks and shovels to scrape and dig. Brushes to wipe away all the obfuscating soil and superstition and surreal stories. So he was good because he didn't think he was better. But maybe the doctor had better tools.

The second part of the dream scared the goodness straight out of the doctor. An evil wind had stirred And he'd awoken in a state of sweat and shivers. A grinding above like the sound of fitful teeth in sleep. He stood up in his bed, placed a hand to the ceiling and quieted his breaths. The grating stopped and he stood in his smalls, knock-kneed and shimmering in humid terror. And then jumped to the floorboards and righted himself as if on a ship tossed on warring waves. He breathed easier and let the echo of the memory of that grating in the ceiling ring from the bone in his head.

Those hands had crashed him through the grasping fronds, into the dark throat that had swallowed the moon. He could barely see but felt all life abuzz and watching, making his skin tingle where he wasn't gripped by fingers, the back of his cudgeled head throbbing and matted with blood. Or so he assumed he must be bleeding since he'd been struck hard enough a second time to fell a rhinoceros. But he wasn't in the plains of this island halfway across the world from his home. He wasn't even sure he was on the main island. It could be Bangka or Belitung for all he knew. But the terrain had gone swampy and the voices were muddled as if they'd climbed up from that morass in a viscous combining of Dutch and Malay and some lost guttural language stretching eons back into the consciousness of the first grunting primates. He was thrown to earth, beyond the bog, past the roots of reaching trees. Shovels struck soil somewhere behind and another set of hands wrenched back his forehead, forcing open his jaws. A great knife with a savage curve glinted from whatever moonlight forced its way through needles and leaves and clasping limbs. That infernal chanting again as fingers fished out his tongue and bit to the teeth. He screamed and showered his assailants in blood. Their grinning eyes, their furrowed brows, their hopping feet to the rhythm of some chthonic dance that always shuddered through the crust of earth, rippling the swamp, shaking the branches overhead, the moon bouncing unseen like an eyeball gouged from an unknown celestial sacrifice. The tongue tossed into the high grass. A hammerfist to the temple and he hit dirt. The omnipresence of ringing bone on metal shovels digging into the remains of past victims and their screams from meatless throats toward an uncaring, vacant sky. He was hauled to his knees as other men dropped burlap bags heavy with clanking, hidden evil—obscured implements of destruction. And the moon closed its bleary eye.

In the lab, later that day, he'd grown irritable. Dr. Sparfield whisked crust from a bone with a small paint brush. The music from the speakers grated on him. The restless spinning fans. The humming of refrigerator units and the running of water. Incessant shakes from the screens, sifting smaller pieces of bone, metal, ceramic, bits of shattered history in a disjointed puzzle. And she always played that album, as if the irony were somehow funny, and maybe it was. But not today, not for Dr. Karkur, when the image of a human tongue callously tossed aside in the bruised cortex of perpetual memory slapped to earth. A pulpy reminder. Remnant. Remains. And from where had Dr. Sparfield gotten that bone?

"Don't you own a different album?" Dr. Karkur had said.

"But I like Alice in Chains."

Dr. Sparfield brushed away like she held the femur to the first known human. Reverence for a being whose speech was barely more complex than preceding hominids. Probably more visible hair than skin. Not far advanced enough for shovels or curved blades. Not complicated enough for ritual and ritual slaughter. Unappreciative of the enormity of just how evil man can be to man. From generation to generation. To pass the knowledge of shipbuilding and sail a hewn and reassembled forest across the globe to commit the basest of acts upon pristine soil. Murder undercover.

Unacknowledged by the Dutch East India Company, for who knows what transpires on the smaller islands of other islands in newly discovered territory? At least newly discovered to this new bright breed of ape. And the bone to that protohuman would shake to be free of the grasp of that greater, smarter, more villainous cousin. Even if it were only Dr. Sparfield. And she wore the mask of a disinterested angel.

"But everyday?" Dr. Karkur had said. "On repeat?"

"You kidding?" she had said. "Them Bones? Dirt? Down in a Hole? That's funny shit."

"Hilarious."

When the doctor had followed the guide through the window to a deeper jungle, he stopped to wipe his glistening brow. At least he guessed it must be shining from all the sun and sweat. Surely, the guide's forehead gleamed like an exhumed diamond that only needed brushed to bring to fullest brilliance. And that guide waved a hand to the doctor and the doctor followed yet again. This was the time when the doctor had still been good and not yet consumed by the constant grating that seemed to be wearing the skull out from the inside. Before he'd brought the stones back. Because the guide had stooped and cleared a clump of grass and pointed with his shining brow at the ground. And there those stones lay, like pulled and discarded molars of a mastodon. Brown and brittle and heaped in a pile. The doctor had stooped, too, and whipped out a brush from his belt to work away at the nearest stone. How had they survived the elements? Sandstone should have long since dissolved. It wasn't as if they'd been preserved in peat. Trapped in resin. Encased in plaster and kept in controlled climate for future curious humans to gawk at. And the doctor, the good doctor still, could tell right off that they came from a ship. Holystones. Meant for scouring. Erasers of the deeds perpetrated by passing feet. Meant for wooden decks not isolated jungle floor.

"Dark, dark days," the guide had said.

He pointed beyond the pile to a solitary stone. A massive piece the doctor had to hunker down to and consolidate his energy to lift. And when he'd flipped that great square stone, a pale green pit viper hissed out with fangs and bunched itself into a spring. The guide had been faster and took the good doctor out of range with a flying tackle. They stood and backed away. Its eyes shimmered and it hissed one last time before slithering into the brush. The doctor adjusted his toolkit and brushed at his jeans.

"I thought those things lived in trees," Dr. Karkur had said.

The guide shook, glanced over both shoulders and said:

"Dark, dark days."

The man had been thrown into the hole. Even if only a dream, Dr. Karkur could smell the damp soil, could feel the slap of it against the legs, midsection and finally chest as they buried the poor bastard alive. But not completely. Up to the armpits. Just enough so that he could only twist his head, dull and full of mountain mist as it was. And with blurred vision he watched as the chanting, stomping, laughing men who'd brought him there unpacked the burlap bags. Small stones and great stones but all square and flat. Holystones for unholy deeds and the man could only scream out inaudibly and spit blood down his chin. Maybe he wanted to yell at the sky for an answer, for surely these monsters masquerading as men wouldn't care to reply. Maybe the man already knew why he was there, why he'd been dragged ponderously through the jungle to suffer an inglorious fate. But the answer, whether known or unknown, wasn't foremost on the victim's mind. It couldn't have been. More likely the desire to stretch out and grasp the knife that was in such tantalizing proximity. Except that his arms were beneath the soil. And the earth couldn't grip tight enough to choke the very life from him. Just hard enough to ensure immobility. And in that frozen state he watched in helpless horror as those monsters as men picked up the smaller stones, hefted them and chuckled, before flinging them full force to his head and body. Prayer books pelting. Heavy thudding rain. Fat projectiles rocking the buried human in place. One glanced off the forehead and snapped the head back, but not enough to bring about merciful release. Buffeted and bleeding and cracking with each collision. Showering imprecations unheard but seen in flecks and froth of blood. Curse you, curse you, curse you felt the doctor in the reverberations of his battered head. Pulped and tongueless and barely able to see through the tears as one man stalked up with a great big bible of a stone above his head, arms shuddering from the weight, and that monster rock crying down as it blotted out what little was left of the light of the moon.

The doctor opened his eyes to darkness and heard the ringing of the doorbell. Had there been a grating above his head or was he only grinding his teeth again in sleep? He shot up and out the room, down the hallway to answer the door. There'd been an appeal, he'd swear to it on a stack of bibles. On a pile of holystones. But no one was there. And when he'd closed the door, just before metal kissed lintel, the sound of escaping air, or collapsing air, made him spin on his heels. The hissing of the pit viper but the snake wasn't there either, of course. He wasn't in Sumatra. He didn't live in a tree. Even though he knew arboreal snakes would come to earth, spring from branches, to cover and coil around prey. But there was no coiling in his lair. Just a tightening in the chest, maybe, and he couldn't help but think how grateful the buried victim in the jungle would've been if he'd had a heart attack before the stones came thundering down. He returned to his bedroom but refused to look at the ceiling. For once, the archaeologist was afraid to dig deep into mystery. For once he'd leave those bones to lie in the tall grass. Or wherever the remains had gotten to—been carried to — dissolved into. Because in the surrounding domain where the guide had shown the doctor the holystones, there'd not been one bone recovered. Not a femur or skull or rib or tooth. Nothing human except the evidence of transport from one human destination to another. From ship to forest. From the nether lands to the eastern islands. And the biggest rock, the greatest cornerstone to this absurd mausoleum, this temple in shambles guarded by a serpent, had what appeared to be a bloodstain soaked into its entire backside. Now with the dreams he knew where the blood had come from. But what about the bones? And those absent remains bit into flesh like the curved fangs of a disturbed viper.

"Did you know that they used salt water and sand to scrub the decks?" Dr. Karkur had said to Dr. Sparfield. "With the stones."

"And?"

But she hadn't looked up. Just crinkled her nose and stared behind her glasses at a crack in a fragment of pottery in her hands. She blew at the object and rolled her head from right to left. Like the head of a dancing cobra before a strike. Except that the snake had been a Sumatran viper. And, of course, Dr. Sparfield was a human. With very real human curiosity. Dr. Karkur couldn't help but wonder if she'd roll her head the same way at a man buried in soil and being stoned to death.

"You know," Dr. Karkur had said. "I kept one of the stones."

"What?"

And she turned to face him, one hand poised with the fragment for another blowing, the other around the handle of a brush. She looked as if she'd like to take a soil core sampler to Dr. Karkur's chest and find out just what exactly was wrong with him — what was buried deep within. Plunged into the heart of a strange new tell and ready to plumb the depth. Maybe cursing herself for keeping the camera on a table in another room.

"It's in the attic, in my house," Dr. Karkur had said. "An unusually large stone with . . ."

But the doctor, who'd become less and less good over the days filled with dark dreams, had stopped himself. She didn't need to know about the blood. Or the stain on the stone, rather, because he couldn't confirm exactly what had discolored the surface. No scientific tests had been run on that singular holystone. Just hidden again in another tomb. But restless, he'd swear, since he always heard the thing grinding down wood like rats in a wall. Wearing his patience thin. Eroding his curiosity. Crumbling the walls, or floor rather, to any scientific methodology the not-so-good doctor would have previously employed.

"You have to bring it in," Dr. Sparfield had said.

"You'll have to come get it."

"Why?"

Because he was scared shitless. After all those screwy, bloody, horrifying dreams. But he answered untruthfully, as all not-so-good persons will do.

"It's really heavy."

The Malay guide had said he'd help carry the stones back to the vehicle at the jungle's edge. But that was it. That's where the relationship would end. After many declarations of dark, dark days and blood on the decks and blood in the water, the guide had walked off toward his skiff on the shore and pushed himself to freedom. Dr. Karkur could only look on, an Isuzu full of stones that were meant for a ship from centuries ago which would be loaded onto a different ship from the current century and sent to the new world with their ancient secrets embedded into sandstone. And the ugly red birthmark on the back of the biggest stone. Maybe a map to a grand new continent. A dark continent. A boundary marker to the habitation of purest evil. And that evil soon to be resting its bulk on the floor of the doctor's attic. But he hadn't known it at this point. And yet he shook as if a cold wind had just whistled through every bone of his being. And that whistling phased into a murmur, a chanting, a grinding of teeth and a grinding of wood. For all eternity, because this great rock could simply never be worn down. And the good doctor, as of this point still, shook again and whistled to rid the memory of the pale green snake that had slunk to the forest floor like water down the drain to an abyss.

But then, now, there was no dream. Just the impression of impending collapse. A rocking cataclysm. Rending plaster and cracking bone. Moonlit eyes and teeth gleaming in the jungle. His own bloodshot, bleary orbs widened for a second before the massive holystone crashed down on his never-to-be-good-again head. And in that second he'd wanted to say something, utter a curse or protestation, but his tongue was limp and choking at the back of the throat. As if he'd been bitten by the snake. The venom paralyzing everything except the senses. And all those senses — sight, sound, smell, taste, feel — coalescing for one final crescendo and obliterating his skull in symphonic catastrophe.

Holy, holy, holystone!

When Dr. Sparfield finally came to his house and actually did ring the doorbell and hadn't the need to shoo a snake in the corners of the porch, she opened the door after several minutes since curiosity always overrode protocol in her empirical being, headed down that same hall that he had when he'd thought he'd heard a doorbell but hadn't, and swung a right into his bedroom. There was the stone in the middle of the bed. And it was truly big. And it did indeed appear heavy. Under that great hulk was a jar of exploded strawberry jam. Or so it seemed from the spray on the pillows and drippings from the wall. And stretching out from the monstrous monolith were Dr. Karkur's limbs, unburied in soil, but every bit as unmovable. Shifting that massive rock off the bed was going to be a real pain in the ass, Dr. Sparfield knew. She went up to it and pushed with half her strength. Nothing moved. Not even the striped pajama top caught beneath the edge.

"It is heavy," she had said.

And looked over both shoulders. Whether from the grate of snake skin on wood or stone on a ship's deck or the grinding of teeth Dr. Sparfield would never know. But she couldn't help but stare at where the erstwhile good doctor's head had been because she swore she heard a voice. And chanting. And stomping feet. But she definitely heard someone utter some very distinct words. And she audibly echoed the sentiment.

"Dark, dark days, to be sure."

Mr. Cornbluth's Swizzle Party

Crash the cymbals! It's Mr. Cornbluth's annual swizzle party!

Ring the bells! Strike the bones! Bang the heads! Blow the horns on this illustrious day of days!

Beat the gongs! Grind the spines! Pound the tympani! Blind the eyes on this glorious reign of pain!

Crack the snares! Smash the teeth! Pluck the strings! Slash the weak on this joyous eve of feasting!

Crash! Crash! Crash the cymbals!

Smash! Smash! Smash the weaklings!

Bang! Bang! Bang the bleating!

On this the day, the very best of days, the day to end all days of days!

'Cause it's the —

Amazing

Astounding

Arousing

Carousing

Stupendous

Tremendous

Momentous

You bet it's

Mr. Cornbluth's annual swizzle party!

The guests had all arrived. They ringed the dining table in the center of the room with empty hands. Except for Mr. Cornbluth who held a pipe to his lips. And behind him against the far wall was a cage. And in that cage kneeled a man with fingers clinging to the ferruled mesh. Dark circles under the eyes to match the greater circle of humans around the table. Concentric darkness around darkness and Mr. Cornbluth moved to the dimmer on the side wall and raised the lighting. He returned to the silent ring, removed the pipe and waved it at eye level.

"Welcome one and all!" Mr. Cornbluth said. "To my yearly celebration of man's dominance over all life. Even over man himself."

"Blasphemy," a hooded figure said.

"Quiet." A mutter from another hood.

This being two of five robed bodies in the ring. Heads bowed and hands resting inside opposite sleeves. The rest remained silent as did everyone else in the circle. Their time will come soon to speak. But not now, for Mr. Cornbluth poked out the long black pipestem at the first robed figure who'd spoken.

"I realize that not everyone shares my conviction in the superiority of man over all else," Mr. Cornbluth said and waited for restless feet to stop shifting. "But whether that belief instead rests in beast, twisting demon or minor god among gods—"

"Blasphemy."

"Shut it."

"—it's frightfully good of everyone present to put aside their differences for one night a year," Mr. Cornbluth said, "and revel in the unconquerable darkness that resides within the pounding of each of our hearts." He swiped with the bent stem. "Inside us, outside us, hovering in the ether—no matter. We all came here not to just celebrate dominance, but to ensure that that dominance stays rooted to the throne for all eternity. In ritual. By will and by might." Blue eyes twinkled above the cornflower ascot crushed against his throat. "Again I say, Welcome one and all!"

"All shall quail before Moloch," the first robed figure said in a hush.

"Shut your mouth, Melqart," said the second robed being. "Or I'll shut it for you."

"Please, friends," Mr. Cornbluth said. "Remove your hoods and be comfortable. You must be sweltering under those monastic shrouds."

And Mr. Cornbluth stuck the pipe back into his teeth. He was wearing a thick brown hound's-tooth jacket. Wool with leather patches at the elbows, of course. But you'd never know that great paragon of a bygone nobility to break a sweat, whether on brow or under jacket or around the joints where the darkness seemed to cling to him most—cinch him in tight with silken bonds of perfumed evil. The epitome of poise and polish and preternatural perception. A cobalt shotgun gaze leveled at every being in attendance. Like the flickering eyes of a Siberian husky before deciding to gobble up the pups.

"Thank God," a woman said from a robe. "I'm sweating my balls off."

She brushed back a hood to reveal long black hair. The others like dominoes swept theirs from heads. Five robed figures, still—flushed faces regarding one another with smirks, averted eyes and mopping brows.

"Anat," Mr. Cornbluth said. "You are a vision."

"Just keep your grandpa paws off me this year," Anat said. "Pervert."

"Anat!"

And the tallest of the once-cowled figures nearly growled at her. Red heat blazed beneath his blond buzz cut. Anat sneered. She refused to look down. And so did the man.

"It's of no consequence, Hadad," Mr. Cornbluth said. "I suspect it was her balls doing the talking." And before Anat could reply, Mr. Cornbluth turned to another woman in robes. "And you, Asherah, whose beauty would make Lucifer's tail stand on end. Where is Eshmun tonight?"

"With the babysitter," Asherah said.

"Excuse me?"

"Oh, you mean . . ." And she brushed a long crimson tress behind and ear and blushed to the same color.

"He's in absolute pieces he couldn't be here," Anat said, smirking—ever smirking. "You could say he was cut to the quick."

"Is that so?" But Cornbluth didn't turn to regard Anat.

"Yeah, he was bleeding all over the place," another robed figure said.

Hadad coughed. "An accident, only a mere accident. He'll be fine."

"Fine as dust," Anat muttered.

Hadad glowered at her smirk and her smirk brought up her middle finger.

"Well, in any case," Mr. Cornbluth said, "I'm glad the rest of you could make it." He nodded to a robed young man with curly brown hair. "Melqart, welcome." The young man looked to the floor as Cornbluth spun his majestic head to the remaining unnamed, enrobed woman. "And Qetesh." And so now named. "You've got the most beautiful head. Has anyone ever told you that?"

"That it would make a fine bowl," Qetesh said.

"That it would."

Qetesh batted her long lashes and somewhere the moans of scourged nymphomaniac nuns could be heard ringing down stone corridors. Hadad rubbed her shorn scalp and Anat chuckled. Asherah's face turned fire upon Hadad and Anat while Melqart couldn't be bothered to notice anything other than the stone flags beneath his toes. Yes, his toes, because he was wearing sandals. And yes, sandals, because Melqart was that kind of guy to bring

142

sandals to an abattoir. A pussy, really, as Anat would most likely say, as I'm sure you'd expect if you'd read the first story of this collection. But I digress while Mr. Cornbluth brings it all back into sharp focus with one mighty clap.

"So," he said, holding the ball-shaped bowl of his pipe. "There is one fresh new face here for our grand party of parties. And I'll be keelhauled if I can guess who brought her."

"This is Anassas," said a man with slicked gray hair. "She works for me. Or, rather, for the company."

And the man tucked his well-manicured hands inside the pockets of his black velvet smoking jacket. He had a red vest and black bow tie, so it should be easy to guess just exactly what type of creature this man was. Long fingered wolf in the softest apparel. A filet knife wrapped in a cashmere scarf. An eye tooth filed and gleaming in moonlight before it sinks into shuddering white flesh. Or so you're being told to think so since it saves us all a whole lot of time. Am I right?

"You were right to bring her, Julius," said Mr. Cornbluth, sapphires flashing. "Rarely has such stunning elegance flickered across these weary old eyes."

"Pervert," Anat said.

Asherah rolled her eyes. Maybe at Anat, maybe at Cornbluth, maybe at both. Qetesh crinkled her brow and rubbed her scalp while pouting.

"It's an honor, surely," Anassas said.

And the world stopped for a moment. Pouts, rubs, crinkles, perverts, rollings, flashes all suspended in time. Set to hover like blushes blown-out on metropolitan LED screens. And while that world ceased its major and minor motions, Anassas carried her own as if unimpeded, tossing back her honeyed hair, wafting jasmine round the room in ecstatic circles, green irises that bent all light, pink lips to suck all manic frustration into whimpering submission, and the décolletage to carry the brunt of all that spent frustration. Or so it seemed to Mr. Cornbluth once the flashes returned to his eyes as the earth resumed its rotation.

"Forgive me for staring, Lady Anassas," Mr. Cornbluth said. "But the readers needed to know just how beautiful you truly are."

"Just Anassas," she said. "Anassas Radek."

"Fine, fine."

"Who are the readers?"

A different man from the circle piped up while Mr. Cornbluth puffed away at burgundy briarwood. And this handsome young man posed the only real threat to Mr. Cornbluth's inexhaustible nature. He looked every bit the sheen to a diamond pulled from the lathe. In midnight blue suit and tie that fit like the iridescence to a beetle. Always fresh from the barber so as to be fresh for the bordello. Or so Mr. Cornbluth reckoned it. And he reckoned he must find some viable way to keep this lusty Casanova at bay or else drown him in the canal after smashing his pate with an oar.

"The readers, Mr. Flyte, are those who are fortunate enough to espy the splendor hidden in every fold of Miss Radek's perfect features."

"I think I'm going to vomit," said Anat.

"Stuff it, whore," said Asherah.

"Oh, you'd love me to, wouldn't you," Anat said. "Stuff it like I did with the carrot. Remember?"

And Asherah went beet-red because beets are so red that they're really purple. And speaking of purple, two other guests stood in this ring, if standing it could be called since they seemed more nervous insect than human, clad in royalest of royal purple to make the Carolingians proud. Except those fusty old nobles are long dead and no one cares about them anyway, especially since there's a human in a cage at the back of the room. I mean, what the hell's up with that? In any case, the woman's purple shades seemed to cut through the air, singeing molecules and mosquitoes alike. Sure, tan slacks and a black blouse aren't purple, so it could be an overstatement to say that she was "clad in royalest of royal purple". But those violet lenses seemed to overtake her whole being, really, as if the rest of her flesh were nothing more than puppetry propping up spinning quasars. But the guy next to her, the weirdo with the black leggings and kneepads, he had a purple shirt and purple cycling cap as if a bottle of red wind had burst over his head. Pop!

"Well," said Mr. Flyte, "I doubt the Scatterings are as enamored as you are, Mr. Cornbluth."

Mr. Cornbluth wheeled on his heels and regarded the odd couple who barely seemed capable of standing in a circle without breaking into some sort of arthropodal flitter or sidling. He stroked his salt and pepper goatee. Yes, I forgot to tell you that he had one. Well, it can hardly be faulted with all of these characters to keep track of. See, now I'm ending sentences with prepositions. Yes, yes, shake shake shake it off.

"I can hardly ask the dear Scatterings here to shake hands with Miss Radek since I'm not entirely convinced they're even human." Mr. Cornbluth leaned in and sniffed the air, but all he could smell was the cherry from his pipe. And the honey from the tresses of the lovely Anassas, of course, but he'd resume that preoccupation in due time. All in due time, Mr. Cornbluth!

"Slrrrp sleeemp sleeemp slrrrp," said the woman.

"Shlrrrp shleeemp shlrrrp shleeemp shleeemp," said the man.

And it really could be more faithfully translated as the sound knotted rope makes when pulled through mud.

"Violet and Rayleigh," Mr. Cornbluth said. "Are those even your real names? No, wait." And he held up his hand because he knew no one wanted to hear that blargon again let alone write it.

"I thought this was supposed to be a party," another person from the circle said.

"Quite right!" said Mr. Cornbluth.

And spun toward the woman who'd spoken. You think he'd get tired of all this spinning, Mr. Cornbluth, especially at his age. But he's a randy old cuss and randy old cusses can spin a good long time when there's honey and quim and cherry in the air. Maybe all that spinning, after all these years, after all those parties, is the mystery behind his eyepatch. Oh, yes, sorry to have omitted that bit. But, just imagine how Cornbluth had felt when he lost that eye! And maybe from all that spinning, like I've said. And so now you're spinning, too. Sorry.

"So sorry to not yet have acknowledged the inestimable presence of the great Dr. Sparfield."

"Where are the drinks?" she said.

"Black balls!" Mr. Cornbluth adjusted his eyepatch. "I'd nearly forgotten."

"Maybe you're getting senile," Anat said.

"Let's not lose focus here," Cornbluth said.

And he looked Dr. Sparfield squarely in the eye. Well, as best he could since she was easily the tallest person in the room. Probably played college basketball. Or should have. Jesus, did Cornbluth wonder at how tricky a task it would be to sixty-nine a pony-tailed giant like that. And maybe if the pony tail were unknotted, she'd grow another six inches. And you bet your bullyboy that Cornbluth would grow another six inches as well. Well!

"Well," said Dr. Sparfield. "Where are they?"

"Was your basketball jersey numbered sixty-nine?"

"Pervert," said Anat.

"The drinks?" said Dr. Sparfield.

"Oh, yes." Mr. Cornbluth shook his head, adjusted his eyepatch and stroked his salt and pepper goatee. "The swizzles!"

"What's a swizzle?" Anassas said.

Spinning again, Mr. Cornbluth said, "Yes, yes, exactly. The swizzle. No mere geedunk to be fobbed off on the casual crowd at Christmas time."

"God, I hate Christmas," said Anat.

"But what's a swizzle?" Anassas, beautiful Anassas, always plump and pink and perfect Anassas said.

"Yes, yes, the swizzle," Mr. Cornbluth said. "The calm before the storm. The writhing before the climax. The catastrophe before the collapse."

"You're rambling," Dr. Sparfield said and adjusted her glasses. Of course she has glasses. She's a doctor. Even though nobody notices. Not that she's a doctor. Everyone can tell that, if even a very unusually tall doctor. But no one notices she wears glasses. Until now. But it will be our secret. Don't tell Cornbluth.

"For God's sake," Anassas said. "What is a swizzle?"

"Yes, yes, precisely," Mr. Cornbluth said. "But it's not a thing that can be told but rather shown." He removed his pipe and cocked his head. "You understand?"

"Not a word."

"Why the hell am I in a cage," said the man in the cage.

And then everything got uncomfortably quiet.

Mr. Cornbluth flexed they eyepatch strap and set it snugly back in its orbit. He stroked his salt and pepper goatee (what a man, what a man, what a man, what a mighty good man). He twirled on his heels with the grace of a seasoned dancer, pipe tight and polish gleaming in the light. He stopped and extracted that pipe. And both his blue eyes kept on whipping in circles even though only one of them could be seen. Scintillating sapphires just the same. And he pointed the stem at the man cowering in the cage as Cornbluth's steps brought him ever closer to the meshing. The pipestem stabbed out like he'd sink it into the poor animal's mug and pluck out his eye whole and swallow it down in one gulp — optic nerve and all.

"Well, Carnis," he said, "you're awful vocal for a pile of meat."

147

"Meat," Anat said.

"Meat, meat, meat, meat," said the other four robed members.

"I'm not meat," said the man, cringing. "I'm human."

"Human," Anat said.

"Human, human, human, human," from the other four robes.

And then, "Hail, Moloch!" quietly, weakly from Melqart.

Mr. Cornbluth tapped at the mesh with his stem and the man backed away. And then the host of the bash to end all bashes thrust out that arm with the pipe and exclaimed:

"Raw man-flesh!"

"Man-flesh." Anat.

"Man-flesh, man-flesh, man-flesh, man-flesh." The other four.

"What?" said the man from the back of the cage, which wasn't very far, not far enough for him, not as far as the opposite end of the country, which would've suited him just fine. God, anywhere to be out of reach of these chanting cannibals in a house that seemed far too modern to hold such ancient urges. Hungry Neanderthals. A neo-Leopard Society with claw-like weapons and finely-honed teeth. Crocodiles with snapping jaws and bloody oblong scales. Spinning reptilian eyes, both eyes, even though Cornbluth had one lid permanently locked shut.

"Keep your composure, Carnis," Cornbluth said. "We don't want to put the cart before the horse, jump the shark, leap before we look . . . ah . . . "

And Mr. Cornbluth turned back to the ring around the table, still in a crouch, and implored with his hands — the one grasping the ball of the pipe, the other with fingers stirring air molecules not split by Violet Scattering's searing beams.

"Another analogy, please," Cornbluth said.

And Violet: "Slrrrp sleeemp slrrrp slrrrp."

"No, not you." Cornbluth shook his head.

"Spoil supper with dessert?" said Mr. Flyte.

Even though Cornbluth hated to admit it, since Flyte was his only real threat to bedding the sublime, supreme, shapely Anassas Radek, he nodded and cleared his throat.

"Precisely!"

And he shifted back to the man at the back of the cage. And the man at the back of the cage shifted so he didn't have to look at those spinning blue eyes, even though Cornbluth had the eyepatch.

"You'll be invited to dinner, Carnis, soon enough," Cornbluth said. "Soon enough, indeed."

"My name isn't Carnis," the caged man said.

"Meat," Anat said.

"Meat, meat, meat, meat," from the four in robes.

Mr. Cornbluth stood and faced the table and the expectant faces. Those flushed, those impassive, those curious, those voracious, those bloodless and bloodfilled faces in the room. He was tired of poking out the pipe. Sick of stroking the beard, though not so much as the pipe sticking. And he was bored with the eyepatch twiddling, though not so much as the beard stroking, and certainly not so much as the pipe sticking, since the eyepatch was the last idiosyncrasy introduced. So he twiddled away.

"The drinks?" Dr. Sparfield said.

"The swizzles?" Anassas said.

"Ah, yes," Cornbluth rejoined, and that will be the last speaker attribution to fill these pages. "Page upon page — oh, wait. One moment."

And Mr. Cornbluth left the room through a doorway. Feet shifting, glances shot round the room, awkward scratching and rubbing of scalps — those who had skulls comely enough to be used as votive bowls. But before any other clumsy account of human impatience could be forced on you, dear reader, Mr. Cornbluth returned bearing a tray with steady grace and import. He sat that tray on the table and took a step back. The thought of either pipe stab or beard stroke or patch twiddle seemed to flicker across his features. His noble features. His regal bearing. Merovingian and erect. A cross alisée to the ascot and blinking in silvery sovereignty. But he decided against any affectation and just went the hell on with it already.

"Page upon page of history is filled with witches' brews and philtres and bubbling cauldrons. Snake oil and myrtle berry tea. And every one of those — whether placebo, injurious or fatalistic — could never compare to the Olympian nectar set before you."

Mr. Cornbluth didn't stab, stroke or twiddle and spoke on.

"So, dear readers of the deeper mysteries, you may wonder to yourself what makes these particular potables so bloody special."

But the circle didn't seem to wonder. Impatience more like. There were nods and assents and shrugs all around. Except for maybe Julius who had his crisply-manicured hands buried to the top knuckles in his black velvet smoking jacket. Impassive face as if cut from stone. And maybe he had been. The slate gray hair, the angular cheekbones, the granite visage that seemed to accept all things at their appointed time and only moved when the opportunity suited to do so. But everyone else fidgeted like patients in a dentist's waiting room.

"Well," continued Cornbluth (damn it! speaker attribution). "There's nothing at all special about these drinks themselves except for the momentous act they precede. A pacer, if you will, to the main event. Or the main entrée, I should say."

And Cornbluth chuckled. Though that's not a singular quirk, really. Everyone chuckles at some time. Except for maybe Julius with the blood-red vest and bowtie black as a raven's severed wing. So the chuckling was natural. And the chuckling was good. Because Mr. Cornbluth was such a mighty good man! What a man, what a man, what a mighty good man! And superlative host.

"For some of you," Mr. Cornbluth said, "this event happens only once a year, much like a black Christmas."

"I fucking hate Christmas," Anat said.

"And for some of us—" And here Cornbluth almost went for the eyepatch. Almost. But he forged on as a good soldier down the hill with bayonet upstanding should. "Some of us indulge in the ultimate ambrosia more often." And here Cornbluth winked at Julius with his good eye. "That's what keeps me so hale and virile." And here Cornbluth winked at Anassas and licked his lips circled by that salt and pepper goatee. "But tonight, my dear friends, in robes or frocks or suits or nothing more than the divine skin nature graced you with . . " And he licked his lips again.

"Pervert," Anat said.

"Well, tonight," he said, "we're of the same stripe, cut from the same cloth, spun of the same silk, carved from the same shining diamond pickaxed from blackest earth."

The young Mr. Flyte adjusted the lapels to his midnight blue suit and offered Anassas a wink of his own, which she summarily ignored. But not Mr. Cornbluth. He noticed it, by God! He noticed aright! And so his voice rose in volume as his finger came up to pull all eyes from the brilliantly shining Mr. Flyte.

"Splice the mainbrace!" And Mr. Cornbluth brought together a resounding clap. "Tonight we drink to eternity!"

"What are you going to do with me?" said the man from the cage, to the front and clutching the ferrules as if they'd protect him from impending fate. Impending since nothing could stop it. Hence the usage of the word impending. I mean, this poor fucker is doomed. And to

151

pound that point oh-so-painfully home, Mr. Cornbluth rotated oh-so-slowly, like the tip of a blade separating skin from flesh along the entire flank, and spoke oh-so-nonchalantly to the captive.

"Well, Carnis," he said. "We're going to eat you, of course."

"Here, here," from Julius.

"Meat," from Anat.

"Meat, meat, meat, meat," from the robed four.

And then Qetesh, one of the robed four, as you are well aware, spoke up: "Wait. We don't have to watch, do we?" Disgust crumpled her innocent baby-doll face. "I can't stand the sight of blood."

"You can't eat me!" The caged man's eyes widened and Mr. Cornbluth wondered at how exquisite they'd be popping between his molars.

"We can," said Mr. Cornbluth. "And we shall." And he turned back to the ring, lifted a glass from the tray and said: "And so say all of us."

"And so say all of us!"

All eleven of them answered. Some impatiently, some forcefully, some with a hint of hesitation though it was hardly noted by anyone in the furor at the prospect of human flesh. Raw man-flesh!

"There'll be the devil to pay," the caged man said.

"Quite right, quite right," Mr. Cornbluth said without turning. "And that devil is frightfully hungry."

"But I don't want to die!"

"Hell's bells, my man," said Cornbluth. "Show a little backbone. We all have to die someday."

"Not believers in Moloch." But Melqart said it so quietly that only the flagstones heard him. Well, and of course, you and I.

"You and I and everyone here," said Cornbluth. "Well, except for our nearly departed Carnis here." Chuckles and chuckles, because it was natural. "We'll lift a drink made by special preparation and by my personal

152

overseeing. A little ramboozle for every bright-eyed boatswain and deckhand in the Royal Navy."

"Royal?" Julius said.

"Forgive me." Mr. Cornbluth shook his majestic head. "I forget myself sometimes. As if we're all tossing about on a great ship, about to sail into some blood orange sunset and ride the waves to the Cannibal Isles and butcher the butcher and find out for ourselves just what a cannibal's flesh tastes like. A human on a steady diet of human, by God, that would be the real thing, the showstopper, the marrow buried deep between the devil and the deep!"

"Cannibal flesh, eh?" Anassas said. Beautifully plump and perfect Anassas. And Cornbluth nearly forgot where he was, lost in all that dove-white goddess skin bunched below her uncut throat. Uncut. Uncut. By God, Cornbluth would love to cut that throat and drink the blood while stabbing his pipestem deep into her bowels until the sounding of the bells. Ringing, ringing bells.

"I don't want to be eaten!" The caged man rocked the wire mesh with white-knuckled fury.

"Holy impaled Christ!" And Cornbluth flipped up his patch to let both eyes blare upon the cowering victim. "If you don't cease that infernal racket, I'll have your tongue out and bleeding in my hand."

"Can I have the tongue?" Dr. Sparfield said.

"No fair," Qetesh said. "You had it last year."

"I had her last year," Anat said. "Barely found a carrot long enough."

"What the hell is your fascination with carrots?" Qetesh said.

"They're long and pointy," Anat said. "And full of beta-carotene."

"You disgust me," Qetesh said.

"You clearly are vitamin deficient."

And Rayleigh Scattering: "Shlrrrp shlrrrp shleeemp shlrrrp."

"I think we got off track, Mr. Cornbluth," Anassas said.

And that illustrious host of hosts at the soiree to end all soirees before the feast to end all feasts nodded, flipped back his eyepatch and stroked his goatee twice before speaking. He almost went for the pipe in his breast pocket, but showed fortitude and impeccable mien in refraining from that habitual fingering. Though he'd love to finger that honey-haired, jasmine-soaked, pink and white buxom beauty from the Celtic Otherworld. Or some such mythological pishposh.

"Quite right, Miss Radek." And Mr. Cornbluth bowed, hand on chest, mere millimeters from the pipe, and his one good eye running up and down every atom of Anassas from Parnassus the goddess to end all goddesses on this night of nights where the ultimate flesh of all flesh would be consumed and settle at the bottom of that heavenliest of heavenly creature's belly. So he held aloft his drink and continued his Dark 'n' Stormy litany.

"This in my hand, dear gathered, is the Devil's Bleeding Heart." Mr. Cornbluth grinned and his ivory teeth seemed elated at having been stolen from the treasure houses of the conquered natives. "And for each of you a special quaff in turn."

Cornbluth grabbed another glass with his free hand and held it to the light before passing it to the person to his left. The left hand of darkness, as it were. Jolly good, Mr. Cornbluth! Jolly good!

(Is everyone still with me on this thing?)

"That concoction is for Mr. Julius Perdo," said Mr. Cornbluth. "Chief Risk Officer for Klaxon Corp. The longest attendee to my annual swizzle party." Cornbluth nodded. "To you, sir, I bequeath the Admiral Stinkweed."

It was passed down the line—to the left, to the left—and into the unshaking, well-manicured hands of Mr. Julius Perdo, CRO of Klaxon Corp. Here, here!

"This next potation is for Mr. Fulton Flyte." Mr.

Cornbluth handed it off. "Heir apparent to the Flyte fortune and surely conqueror of many a woman's throbbing heart. Except for Anassas, of course, since she's meant for the gods." Chuckles, chuckles. A right good uppercut that one, Mr. Cornbluth! "It is the Captain Pricklyburr, and may it warm your tongue to the choicest of victuals to come."

"I've got hepatitis!" the man said from the cage. "You don't want to eat me."

Mr. Cornbluth, with stiff upper lip and stay-calm-and-party-on demeanor, plunged ahead with the festivities. That'll show 'em, Cornbluth! Steady on, sir.

"The Dragon Blood Estate to match the fiery tresses of Asherah."

Passed down. Solemn faces. Expectant tongues.

"The Royal Navy Rootwork for Hadad, leader of the sect of Moloch."

Pass it along. Take another one down.

"The Ashanti Brum for the black heart and black hair of Anat the Vindictive."

"You mean Anat, Queen of Carrots," said Qetesh.

"And for you, my dear." Mr. Cornbluth picked up a peach-colored mix and palmed it to the left. "To Qetesh I humbly offer Mount Obeah — and oh how I'd love to see it's nectar swim at the base of that comely skull."

Passed. Accepted.

"To Melqart, staunch defender of Moloch and no one else . . . the Pirate Jimson."

Pass the dutchie on the left hand side.

"To the purple-eyed demon of the deep, I bestow the Doña Santeria." Mr. Cornbluth nodded and she nodded back. And thankfully nothing was seared in her burning vision. "Enjoy, Violet Scattering."

"Slrrrp Sleeemp."

You're straight on winning it, my man! You're the man of the hour, old boy.

"And to her husband, the Five Finger Bumbo." Mr.

Cornbluth wagged a finger and chuckled. "Try not to break it in your tentacles, Rayleigh."

"Shlrrrp shleeemp."

You're bowling them over, right and left. Pass it on the left! On the left. Hup two three four!

"For the tallest member, not just in stature, but in accreditation, the Rumfustian Loco." And here Mr. Cornbluth hesitated in handing over the brew. "Just what exactly is your first name, Dr. Sparfield?"

"Doctor," she said.

"Yes, yes, I've got that. But your given name, my Amazonian lovely."

"My first name is Doctor."

"So then . . ." Mr. Cornbluth blinked and his eyepatch went askew. He adjusted it and went on. Go on, Mr. Cornbluth! Go on! "So you're name is Doctor Sparfield?"

"Dr. Doctor Sparfield, if you please." And that ponytail couldn't have pulled the skin to her face any tighter. Or else the bone would show. "I didn't go through all that training just to be called Miss Doctor Sparfield."

"Of course, of course, my dear."

Steady! Steady on, sir!

"And finally, the newest addition to our Meat Beat Manifesto. The Queen bee of the hive. The tolling bell in the chest of every man who is fortunate enough to set mortal eyes to her. For none is worthy. Even the gods grovel at your pretty pink feet."

"Blasphemy," said Melqart, holding his Pirate Jimson.

"To you, dear, beautiful, enchanting jewel of the dragon's horde, I beg your acceptance, for you to deign grace my ignoble broth with your angelic lips."

"Pervert," said Anat.

"Anassas Radek, of the Olympians and Titans and all the other pantheons throughout the ages, I present this most potent of punch, this most intoxicating elixir, this hangover-to-end-all-hangovers, the Two Jacks Cane."

You've got her now, Cornbluth. Netted in your wily plans! You'll bed her surely, or my name isn't . . . Well, that's unimportant. Good form, old man! Great blunderbuss of a show!

"And so now, all, glasses raised, heads high and eyes bright as the sun." Mr. Cornbluth the statue on the tippy-tip of the temple. "Let us drink with all haste and not further prolong our dear guest of honor's stay than is necessary." Cornbluth turned back and winked at the man in the cage. "To Carnis!"

"Carnis!"

"Meat," from Anat with Ashanti Brum.

"Meat, meat, meat, meat."

"I don't want to be eaten." The man rested his doomed forehead against the wire, looking down. "Kill me if you must, but please don't eat me. I beg of you."

"My good friend, Julius," Mr. Cornbluth said, after draining half his Bleeding Heart. "Do we appear to be the sort to be moved by begging? By tears? Can gods heed the pleas from fleas on dogs?"

"Blasphemy."

Julius Perdo drained his Stinkweed to the lees. Stone-chiseled and twinkling like a geode in the desert. That rock cracked and spoke:

"Begging does make the meat taste better."

"Indeed," said Cornbluth. "Indeed it does. And what else makes the meat more palatable?"

"Just the right dollop of desperation."

"Brought about from the knowledge that you're going to die?"

"Surely." And now Perdo's face didn't even seem to budge—lips not part and speak. Yet speak he did. "Especially when that flesh is cut from a suicide."

The man from the cage lifted his gaze from the floor, meshing indented along the top of his forehead. A mark of Cain, or Carnis, rather. But no one was here to protect him. No god of Canaanite manufacture or otherwise (Hail Moloch!). More of a brand denoting ownership of that meat. And the caged man's animal heart beat hard enough he maybe hoped it would burst. As all caged hearts before the feast.

"Suicide?" the man said.

And now Cornbluth polished off the remainder to his own Devil Heart. Uncaged. And spun. With jackboot precision. And regarded the branded man through the empty glass.

"Does the meat speak?"

"It speaks," said Anat.

"It speaks, it speaks, it speaks, it speaks," the four.

Mr. Cornbluth gently set that exhausted glass to the tray, behind him, without taking sight off the huddled and shaking man.

"If it speaks," said Cornbluth. "Then it must be man."

"Man-flesh," Anat.

"Man-flesh, man-flesh, man-flesh, man-flesh."

Mr. Cornbluth stuck the tip of an index finger in his mouth. Maybe a drop of the Devil's Bleeding Heart. Maybe preparatory to pushing that digit through the wire mesh, through the ribcage of the doomed man, and straight into the rapidly beating muscle to feel the vibrations in that fight for life rock deep down to his own marrow. Exquisite, pulsing meat, eh, Cornbluth? Right so! Right so!

"And if it be man and in cage," Cornbluth said, "then it must be eaten."

"Meat."

"Meat, meat, meat, meat."

"And if that man willingly give up his own life." Cornbluth bent down again, peering into the face of desolation. "Then that be the sweetest meat of all."

"Oh, sweet, sweet meat of the suicide." And here Julius Perdo actually shook. Like a devil or freezing wind ran across his own granite heart.

Fingers released from ferrules. The man rubbed the top of his forehead while looking straight back into Cornbluth's eyes. Or eye, rather, since the patch was secure, dead and uncaring. And oddly enough, a smile broke upon that face. And after the smile a chuckle. And it was natural, you can be sure of that, Cornbluth. It was a natural enough chuckle all right. And then into chortling before sprinting full force into laughter, head back as far as it can go in a cage, eyes squeezed tight and leaking water like he'd been struck by the staff of Moses. Staff of Moses? Well, the man is in a wilderness of sorts, I guess. And the dark intelligence of a future feasting of one's own flesh by others would hit pretty hard, smote as the Bible would have it, like a wooden staff to the stretched-out bones that couldn't pull away. Because of the cage. And maybe this man knew the secret to why the caged bird sings. Or laughs, rather. Oooooh. Lowbrow, Mr. Cornbluth. Come on, man, you're made of finer stuff than that!

And when that man stopped laughing long enough to open eyes upon Cornbluth's nonplussed face:

"You think I'm going to kill myself?" He shook his head of doom. "I'm not doing your work for you, you lazy bastard."

"You will," said Cornbluth.

"You will, indeed," said Julius Perdo from the far end of the table.

"You can kiss my dick," said the man.

"Can I kiss it?" Anat said, waving.

"Meat, meat, meat, meat."

"Slrrrp sleeemp."

"Shlrrrp shleeemp."

Mr. Cornbluth stroked his salt and pepper goatee. And this was very natural, for he did it abstractedly almost. Still staring into the eaten-man-to-be's eyes, but not really staring at him. As if seeing him as a series of steaks and fillets more than any kind of composite being. And the sum of its parts would add up to so much more than the sorry creature cowering before Cornbluth. And Cornbluth knew this because he'd had the ecstasy of human flesh between his very human teeth. And that rarest of delicacies would not be denied him merely because the man protested at being eaten.

"We will cut you off in pieces," Cornbluth said, hands clamped lightly. "One by one. A foot here, a hand there. And we'll eat those bits of you while you watch."

"Cornbluth, no," said Julius Perdo.

"Can I have his dick?" said Anat.

"And we'll stretch this butchery out until you beg us for death." Cornbluth licked his bottom lip. "But death won't come—not at our hands. And that's when you'll pray for the grace to kill yourself." He flipped up his eyepatch and let the blue cutting wheels bite. "But there won't be enough of you to finish the deed. No hands, no feet, no arms or legs."

"Too far, Cornbluth," Julius said. "You'll spoil the meat."

"Yeah," the caged man said. "You mustn't spoil the meat."

"Meat, meat, meat, meat."

"So the lactates will make you a bit more pungent." Mr. Cornbluth shrugged. "You'll still taste better than any animal felled and consumed that's roamed this planet for eons—since before we humans had the ken, the spurt in brain power, to turn our fear into sharpest flint on the end of a stick, by dint of hard work, superior intelligence, and the stamina to run down any creature on this green, spinning planet, flecked with foam and panting, begging for it to be killed." Cornbluth leaned close enough to smell the doomed man's sweat on terror-slicked skin. "And that's when we march it off the cliff. It jumps to its own destruction. With gratitude. With honor."

"You're seriously fucked in the head," the man

said. But he swallowed hard and leaked from the eyes again. But he wasn't laughing. He wasn't laughing at all, was he, Cornbluth?

"Language, dear Carnis." Cornbluth straightened his hound's-tooth jacket. "There are ladies present."

"So now I know what a swizzle is," said a voice from behind and Cornbluth knew that mellifluous voice to flow from none other than the stateliest of Queen bees, the ruler of the hive, the stunning visage that launched a thousand workers into the fields to wage war with rival colonies upon the vivid hearts of flowers. "When do we eat?"

"Ah, yes, yes, Anassas." Mr. Cornbluth raised a finger to the air. "It's high time we kicked this party up a notch, wot?"

Cornbluth pulled a large curved knife from the inside of his jacket, waved it before the man in the cage, backed up a few paces and laid it on the floor. Backed up to leave enough room for the swinging door, which it did once he unlocked the cage. Still crouching and fanning his hands toward himself. But the man inside the cage refused to stir. The voices of all those around the table were still. No one sipped. No one spoke. No one coughed or offered accusations of blasphemy or perversion or spoilage of meat. And that meat finally answered Cornbluth's silent summons. Hesitant and sweating. Carnis though not Carnis yet meat just the same. From out of the prison and into an even more confining reality. He stood and stretched and the bones in his legs and back cracked as if tossed in a campfire. Cornbluth straightened himself as well—toe to toe with the once-caged pre-consumed man of the doomiest of dooms. Doomiest? Well, yes. How much deeper can this man slip into the abyss? Possibly the digestive tract and finally the anuses of every fine young or old cannibal present at this doomiest of doomed dinners. But he'd hardly be aware of that. Long since dead, flayed and cut into pieces. Long since chatted about how

161

good his flesh was, after all, after he'd finally been convinced to do himself in. Like a good gent, like a good gent, Mr. Cornbluth. Upstanding chap, after all. And after all the edible morsels had been ingested, he'd be no more than a memory — the memory. For all twelve decadent humans. To be fondly remembered before drifting to sleep or at barbecue get-togethers or while unfolding sandwiches in wax paper with inferior meat. And the constant comparison to that succulent flesh of the caged man nearly a year ago and only days before the new would-be suicide to be hunted, caged and forced to take knife to neck and slit his own thankful throat. And the funny thing is, it wasn't the worst of ways to be remembered. The ghost of Carnis would live on in the taste buds and flavor centers of the tongues and brains of each murdering son of a bitch here. So he could think of better ways to be remembered. And reached for the knife.

"Glad to see you've come to your senses," Mr. Cornbluth said.

And like a jackrabbit spring the man was up and out with that curved blade, wild desperate swings. A drunken dervish. A flailing attempt at freedom. But the poor man had been caged so long that his muscles didn't quite react with the precision required. He backed Cornbluth up to the edge of the table, yes, but he'd also left enough room for Hadad to swing over with his meaty fist and crash him a good one to the right eye. Carnis careened into the wall and dropped the knife.

"No!" Cornbluth held up his hands. "You'll bruise the meat!"

Hadad's assault was halted by the steely grip of Dr. Doctor Sparfield. He tried to pull free but only succeeded in spinning himself around to face the good doctor. Well, not face her, of course. But look at the unblemished landscape of her neck. And he followed that snowy landscape to the jut of her chin and downcast sparkling eyes. Hadad didn't even mind that she wore glasses and thought it odd that he hadn't noticed them before.

"You are a mountain of beauty," Hadad said.

The doctor softened her grip as the cliff face crumbled into the ocean.

"Pervert," said Anat.

"Hadad!" Asherah in crimson rage. Or maybe warning. Because Carnis was up on shaky legs again, knife in hand, and advancing toward the couple locked in each other's grip. Oh, love. In the strangest of places, at the strangest of times. Whether before or after consuming man-flesh, love will find a way to worm itself into even the hardest of hearts. But for Cornbluth, it was more about the meat.

"Stay your hand, Carnis!" Mr. Cornbluth pushed away from the table and put himself between Carnis and the enamored couple. "You'll only protract the inevitable. You'll never win. You'll never escape." Cornbluth braved a sweeping gesture behind him at those gathered in the circle. Then back to the man with trembling knife in hand. "There are too many of us. And we're all quite peckish by now. Am I right?"

"Here, here," Julius Perdo said.

"I would've killed him by now," Fulton Flyte said. One of the few with a drink left. So he downed his Captain Pricklyburr and set the empty to the table with a hollow ring. "And, man, I'm more than peckish—I'm starving."

"Famished," said Qetesh.

"I can eat," said Melqart.

"I'm bewitched," said Hadad.

"Ensorcelled," said Dr. Doctor Sparfield.

"Jesus," Anat said. "Get a room."

"So what do you say?" Mr. Cornbluth's arms still out. Head tilted with a twist to the lips. "Be a good sport and slit your throat, eh?"

"You don't want to eat me, I tell you," the desperate man said. "I'd be gamy."

163

"Come on, son."

"I'm an alcoholic."

"You're stalling."

"I eat ghost peppers and fast food."

"Everyone's waiting."

"I just sit around and play videogames all day. I'd be tasteless."

"You'll be just fine."

"I masturbate in the shower."

"Who doesn't."

"I'd get lodged in your throats and . . ."

Carnis who was not Carnis but most surely will be eaten dropped his head, his shoulders and the knife. Again. Hope there's not a nick in the blade, right, Cornbluth? The meat wouldn't be kosher then. Wouldn't want to offend the guests.

"I can't win," he said.

"Exactly what I've been telling you."

"And I don't want to suffer."

"Who does?"

"May as well just make it quick and painless."

"Well . . . quick, yes."

"There is no pain in death."

"It only hurts to die."

Wasn't that from Quicksand? Jesus, sure hope I don't get hit with plagiarism. It's hard enough to keep track of twelve characters without ripping someone else off. Well, thirteen characters counting Carnis. And that thirteenth character put the biting end of the blade against his neck.

Yes. Yes. Yes.

Meat. Meat. Meat. Meat.

And a swizzle we will go!

"Wait!"

Crash the cymbals!

Ring the bells!

Beat the gongs!

164

"Don't!"

Crack the snares!

Blow the horns!

Pound the timpani!

"I've got a better idea," Anassas had said. And the flush in her face was all the evidence needed for the first two interruptions. And who wouldn't "wait" and "don't" or hear her better idea when trumpeted from the milk and honey majesty that is Miss Anassas Radek of Parnassus?

Who indeed, Mr. Cornbluth.

So all turned to this interrupting goddess. All awaited her decree. Or desire. Or whatever it would take to land that mind-numbingly gorgeous Aphrodite squarely into their bed. A roomful of jasmine and a bellyful of honey and an eyeful of paradise forever painted in the distance. A trompe l'oeil that you'd willfully be fooled by. A false reality gratefully accepted. A virtual lie that you wouldn't mind telling yourself over and over if you'd at least hear it from her lips now and again. A perfect disaster for exhausted muscles. A wasting infinity of silk and sacred shivers. To breathe one's last at the foot of the mountain. The holy mountain. And from that mountain, from the rock itself, bursting forth that ineffable shape of beauty to kiss and hiss with tender lips and fire.

Snap out of it, Mr. Cornbluth!

"A tastier idea," Anassas said.

Cornbluth spread his lips wide. Unconsciously stroking the beard and twiddling the eyepatch. Even pulling out the pipe to lance the air all round. As if enchanted for he was enchanted as enchanted as a man of his age could be enchanted and so enchanted he could barely speak as if set face to face with an angel.

"Yes?" he said to that angel.

"You got one to thinking."

"About what, my dove?"

And now Anassas was the one to lick her lips.

"About the flesh of a cannibal," she said.

"Excuse me?'

"What you said about human on a steady diet of human."

"Well." Mr. Cornbluth frittered with his patch and blinked with his good eye. "I get carried away sometimes — over extend myself from time to time — indulge in badinage for the very sake of it. Take no stock in the prattling of an old, I mean refined, man."

"I'm sorry, Mr. Cornbluth, but I just can't shake that image from my mind."

"Just a dream, surely." Cornbluth cleared his throat, which was unnatural, because he just couldn't get what he needed from messing with the eyepatch. "Visions of the future, perhaps. One day maybe to traverse this globe in search of the perfect, the most primal specimen and carve his flesh while running." And he shook his head, but that didn't work either. So he went back to trying to swallow that fat spider that sat on his epiglottis. "You can come with me, my dear, and taste the tabooed delights of the midnight world."

Anassas took a step toward Cornbluth. She had no need to fidget. No desire to clear a throat unobstructed. Her gaze was even and deadly. Cobra eyes. Flicking tongue. But only because it was natural. A very natural thing for a snake to do. And even now, at her suggestion, at where he knew this conversation was inevitably heading, Mr. Cornbluth found her intoxicating. Almost as if he were only two snake-hooded shakes away from caving in and letting those fangs prick his well-bred flesh.

"But why dash halfway around the world," she said, "when we've got all the human-fed homo sapiens right here? In this room."

And now Cornbluth backed up.

"Now hold a minute, my pet," he said. "I was rambling. Merely rambling."

Steps toward the host. His arms up. Leather elbows and an eyepatch. A briarwood pipe and much pulled-upon goatee. Weak defense against a poisonous snake. Weak defense, indeed, Cornbluth. Watch out!

"And if you killed yourself, sweet Mr. Cornbluth." Eyes closed for only a moment with the entire body trembling slightly. Opened and advancing again. "How exquisite — how rare — that meat would be."

"She makes a valid point," Julius Perdo said from the far side of the circle.

Cornbluth's eye opened wide. Blue blazing gem. Winking from the horror under the lights. He held out his arm and pointed the pipe at Julius. But he wasn't a snake. He was a human who ate human. And he knew he was far too human to spring past that slithering beauty, past all the guests ringed round the table, to vault the length of that table and plunge the long black pipestem into the thin chest of the Chief Risk Officer of Klaxon Corp. Alarm! Alarm! But the bobbies weren't coming. There was nothing to protect and serve. Except the rarest of rarest meats at the blowout of all blowouts from the patron saint of anthropophagy: Mr. Cornbluth himself!

"You eat man-flesh far more often than I, Julius!" he said.

"Man-flesh."

"Man-flesh, man-flesh, man-flesh, man-flesh."

"Take him!" Pointing and backing away. "Julius Perdo's flesh would be so much more succulent. So much more decadent. So much more savory than the fusty fare I usually dine upon." Still backpedalling. To nowhere. Except the sidewall. "Waifs and street urchins and drug addicts. You don't want me, I say. You want a far more discriminating host body. The succulous bits of an opulent man who only dines on the fattest of cherubs — the choicest of chattel." And now his heel backed into something solid. And that solid thing was the foot of Carnis. And his uplifted face was beaming with the prospect of hope untasted. "Julius would be Kobe beef. I'd be cube steak, at best." Mr. Cornbluth put hand to chest.

"You don't want this dried-out old jerky."

"You forget that Anassas works for me," Julius said. "You wouldn't want her unemployed now, would you?"

"I like my job," Anassas said.

"You'll find another," Cornbluth said. Barely croaked out, rather. So I guess I could've said "Cornbluth croaked", but I wanted to avoid the unnecessary speaker attribution. Like I said I'd do. And then not have to go into a lengthy defense as to why I avoided the attribution. But then I did. And here we are.

"Here we are, Mr. Cornbluth," Anassas said. "All here for you—for your event—for your pleasure—a thing to celebrate." She reached out before he could stop her and gently tugged on that salt and pepper goatee. "Let's not ruin the festivities by being stingy." She stabbed at the stone floor. "Hand me that blade, Carnis."

The oh-so-recently-caged man bent down and came up with the handle gripped tight as if by the coils of a stick-poked snake. And Cornbluth went to his knees, flipped up his eyepatch, clamped his hands and implored the goddess before him, who now held that curved knife, to not eat him, please God no, to please not feast on his withered carcass.

"Carnis," she said, still blaring down upon the dethroned host of hosts. "I still have some of my drink left. Go join the circle and finish it off. Your name is now Carnivore."

"Meat-eater."

"Meat-eater, meat-eater, meat-eater, meat-eater."

"No, Anassas." Cornbluth's cobalt crushed and streaming down the cheeks. "I made the Two Jacks Cane especially for you."

"Knock if off," she said. "You'd fuck anything with the patience to wait for you to get it up."

"Pervert," said Anat.

Anassas passed the knife to the kneeling

Cornbluth.

"Oh, God," Qetesh said. "There's going to be a lot of blood."

"Here, here!" from Julius Perdo.

"I want the tongue," Dr. Doctor Sparfield said.

"It's my turn this year." And Qetesh pouted.

"Well, then," said Dr. Doctor Sparfield. "You'll have to stay through the bloodshed." And kissed Hadad full on the mouth. So, she still got a tongue in a way.

Oh, ho! Mr. Cornbluth. Good one that, eh? Mr. Cornbluth? Come, come, my man. You stormed the beach of Normandy! You braved the quivering spears of the Zulu! You were wounded by a Russki's musket ball in the Crimea! You fought off scurvy and dysentery and yellow fever. You've been beset by Pygmy savages and Bengal tigers. You've gone hand and tomahawk with the wild Apache outside desert hovels. You've climbed the Pyrenees and swum with crocodiles in Lake Nasser. You've heard the banshee wail and the howl of wolves on the steppes. You've been to the moon and the bowels of the earth. You've been to Sirius and Rigel and strained the stardust of Andromeda. You, sir, are a liar! A confounded, incorrigible, loose-tongued propounder of preposterousness! And now your tongue — yes, your tongue, Mr. Cornbluth — will be severed and feasted upon on this bloodiest of bloody nights.

"Do the right thing, Mr. Cornbluth," Anassas said. "And make this a swizzle party to remember."

And when Cornbluth raised the blade to his throat he paused to see if anyone would stop him. No one did. Everything was hushed. Except for the lip-and-tongue wrestling between Dr. Doctor Sparfield and Hadad. And the palm on scalp rubbing of Qetesh. And the twisting sound of tentacles in mud reaching for prey. Sleeermp shleeemp. And Melqart muttering, "Moloch, Moloch, Moloch." And Asherah's blood boiling. And Fulton Flyte endlessly polishing and straightening his lapels. And Anat fishing in the depths of her robes for a carrot, maybe. And the gasp as Carnis, I mean Carnivore, drained off the rest of the Two Jacks Cane and slapped it back to the table. But other than all that, it was pretty quiet.

"But it's my party," Mr. Cornbluth said, goatee hanging over the dull side of the blade. "And I can do what I want to."

"You can cry," Anassas said. "But this party is no longer yours."

Anassas winked at Mr. Cornbluth. She reached down and flipped back his eyepatch — adjusted it. Smoothed out his goatee. Took his pipe from his other hand and gently stowed it away in the breast pocket. She straightened up and smiled. And those lips parting were like the very heavens opening in the sky, golden shafts probing the plebian plateau of Cornbluth's cold stone floor, lancing his ancient beating heart. He winked back with his unpatched eye.

"You'll have mighty big shoes to fill," Mr. Cornbluth said.

"This party is now the express property of Klaxon Corp," Anassas said, still smiling.

"God, I hope it doesn't get all commercial," he said.

"Never fear, Mr. Cornbluth." She folded her arms. "We're on a whole new trajectory."

"I'll never know what cannibal tastes like," he said.

Don't mistake his weeping for weakness. Though he is kind of a pussy. Right, Anat?

"Pussy," Anat said.

Mr. Cornbluth just wasn't used to missing out on the party. He created the party. He was the party. But, in with the young, out with the old, eh, Cornbluth?

"Your sacrifice will usher in a whole new era," Anassas said.

She turned and that movement sent waves of honeysuckle straight over the blade into the distended nares of Mr. Cornbluth. Better than the cold steel and hosed blood before getting the bolt in the skull. Am I right, Cornbluth? It could be worse. The oh-so-fashionable Fulton Flyte could be making love to the largest cut from the Great Star of Africa on his corpse. And he'd be too dead to hear her sweetclovered moans.

To those encircled swizzlers she said:

"Let's hear it for Mr. Cornbluth!"

"Here! Here!"

And she clapped and they all started clapping. The applause was deafening. At least to a man on his knees with a knife pressed against his neck.

"Mr. Cornbluth!"

"Good show!"

"Good form!"

Good riddance.

Good God.

Good night.

Well, Mr. Cornbluth. You had a good run.

But now it's time to choke on your own blood.

Choke on your pride.

And kiss the knife edge of eternal sleep.

Rather a shame, though, to ruin that beautiful cornflower blue ascot.

Clap clap clapping.

Clash the cannibals!
Grind the gongs!
Splinter the cymbals!
Scream the song!
Of the final swizzle for Mr. Cornbluth!
Drink the blood!
Eat the flesh!
Scoop the brains!
Don't you fret
For the final swizzle of Mr. Cornbluth!
Strip the hide!
Crush the bones!
Pop the eyes!
Now you know
It's the final swizzle for Mr. Cornbluth!
Howl the dogs!
Rend the teeth!
Gobble them all!
In the keep
Of the final swizzle of Mr. Cornbluth!
Clash! Clash! Clash! the cannibals.
Smash! Smash! Smash! the animals.
Crash! Crash! Crash! the carnivores.
Blast! Blast! Blast! the vagabonds.
On this final day, the very best of days, the day to end all days, 'cause the party of parties is happening today!
[ALL TOGETHER]
It's the final swizzle for Mr. Cornbluth!

Aftermath

I'd meant to publish another novel before this collection of short stories. But that endeavor proved too dark and taxing at the time. To avoid a preoccupation with death and destruction over several months, I decided instead to write a series of humorous stories about . . . well, death. (Ah, my old friend.)

So first off, I'd like to acknowledge death. Thanks for all the pant-shitting, life-scarring, mind-frying moments.

Secondly, I'd like to thank Christopher Fielden and the gang helping him with the 'To Hull & Back' Short Story Competition.* Without that, I may not have found the need to string these absurd tales into a coherent whole — a greater absurdity — an absolute abdominal punch that missed and hit instead that absurdly bloated nut sack of life.

Third, to Jamie for proofing this puerile drivel. And for letting me force her to write three lines in a story about a devil baby with a lazy eye.

And lastly, all appropriate kowtowing and ritualistic cutting to my wife who is actually a goddess in a very real, ever-tripping human form. Your artwork, book layout and support are a constant font of inspiration. (And your human form's not too shabby, either!)

So I hope you've enjoyed reading this silly little collection as much as I enjoyed writing it. Unless you've skipped to this part — then you're just a clump of bleu cheese that's been behind the fridge for way too long. You really should get a friend to help move it and clean that foul mess up.

And thanks to me for not having patience for all things boring.

Includes three stories submitted in the second year of the competition. An epic fail!

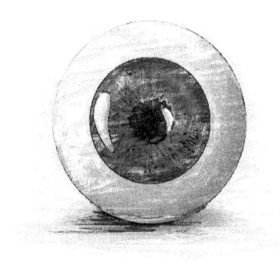

Made in the USA
Columbia, SC
06 July 2019